COAL DUST AND DREAMS

The Story of a Girl and Her Pit Pony in
the Coal Mines of Wales

M.J. Evans

Dancing Horse Press

Foxfield, Colorado

M.J. Evans/Dancing Horse Press
7013 S. Telluride St.
Foxfield, CO 80016
www.dancinghorsepress.com

Publishers Cataloging-In-Publication Data
Name: M.J. Evans, Author
Title: Coal Dust and Dreams/ M.J. Evans
Description: Foxfield, Colorado: Dancing Horse Press / Interest Age Level: 11 and up / Includes Bibliographical references. / Summary: The mining of coal in Wales had a long history of using both children and horses in the extraction process. Entire villages depended on the coal mining industry. This difficult and dirty job was extremely dangerous for both the miners and the horses who helped them. A young Welsh girl goes to work in the local mine when her father is severely injured. Her love of horses takes her 2,000 feet underground as she takes the place of her father as a haulier. / Subjects: Horses – Wales – Pit Ponies – Coal mining – Children in Coal mines.

Ordering information: Contact the address above for special discounts on quantity sales.

Coal Dust and Dreams/M.J. Evans. -- 1st ed. ISBN: 978-1-73736188-6

Praise for "Coal Dust and Dreams"

"Coal Dust and Dreams: The Story of a Girl and Her Pit Pony in the Coal Mines of Wales, is a marvelous work of historical fiction that will teach young readers about the valuable work of pit ponies and those who cared for them. A simple, yet powerful story.
Emily Jane Hills-Orford – Readers' Favorite Book Reviews

M.J. Evans spins a captivating yarn that animal lovers are bound to love. Bethan and Dobbin's bond is at the center of an enthralling narrative that incorporates real-world historical events. These are the kind of stories that brighten your day and put a smile on your face. Recommended to readers who love coming-of-age stories.
Wishing Shelf Book Reviews (UK)

Coal Dust and Dreams may initially attract horse-crazy girls interested in horse stories, but to limit it to that audience would be to do the story a grave disservice. Its real-world background history, social and cultural insights, and lessons on perseverance, problem-solving, and confronting prejudice all give *Coal Dust and Dreams* a supercharged injection of value beyond the usual girl-and-horse tale.
Diane Donovan – Midwest Book Reviews

Contents

When I was a pit-pony driver

Just a boy all alone in the dark

In the dirt and the damp

With a smokey oil lamp

My one grain of comfort was Spark.

There was something about that wee pony

On which I could always depend.

Like the bond between

Shepherd and sheepdog

Or cowboy and four-legged friend.

I remember the first time

That my lamp went out.

The darkness was blacker than night.

I clung to Spark's tail,

Knowing he wouldn't fail,

And he led me right back to the light.

(From the poem "Spark" by J.R. Green, Doncaster)

M.J. Evans

Chapter 1

A few miles north of Caerphilly, South
Wales, August 1997

The thunderous roar of the engines powering the enormous earthmovers drowned out all other sounds. A short distance away, an old woman tightly clutched the hand of her granddaughter, both fixated on the transformative spectacle unfolding before them – a shifting mound of coal slag.

"What are they doing, Mamgu?" the girl asked, curiosity lighting up her sparkling green eyes. Her voice was lost in the cacophony.

The grandmother bent down. "What did you say, my child?"

Quinn, bearing the name that showed her father's Scottish heritage, rose on her toes and shouted into her grandmother's ear. "I said 'What are they doing?'"

The woman nodded as she straightened up. "They're fashioning a monument out of the slag heap, what remains of the coal mine over which we stand. It is meant to be a monument in remembrance of the pit ponies. When they are done, it will be an enormous mound of slag, sculpted to look like a running horse. Its mane will be thick ridges and its tail will appear to flow out behind it."

She paused for a moment to wipe a tear from her eye. Having composed herself, she continued. "When it is completed, a hiking trail will run from the tip of its nose, across its spine, and down one leg all the way to the end of its hoof. Hikers can rest on benches that will be placed in one of its nostrils and ears. We locals have decided to name it 'Sultan' after one of the pit ponies who is still alive."

The roar of the earth movers filled the air again.

"Of course," she said with a chuckle when the engines had quieted a bit, "the entire earthen sculpture will be best seen from an airplane."

"Pit ponies?" Quinn's head cocked to one side, her curiosity piqued.

A veil of nostalgia clouded the grandmother's gaze, and a second tear traced a path down her weathered cheek. With a gentle squeeze of Quinn's hand, she said, "Let me tell you about the pit ponies and your proud Welsh heritage you have inherited from my daughter."

The old woman led her granddaughter across a grass-covered field to a wooden bench that had been carefully placed beside a newly planted tree. She sat down, looked up at Quinn, and patted the bench. "Sit, and I will unravel the tales of these unsung heroes."

Chapter 2

The girl rubbed the sleep from her large hazel eyes as she rolled over in her bed. A pale ray of morning sunlight worked its way between the ragged burlap curtains and spread across her pillow. Beneath her attic room, the girl knew her mother was preparing breakfast. She would be calling for her soon.

She stretched her young body and worked her feet out from under the blankets. As she looked down, her long light-brown hair fell over her face. Brushing it back with her hands, she wiggled her dainty toes and smiled. "Time to get moving, feet," she giggled.

The smell of frying bacon wafted up from the kitchen as the child put on her grammar school uniform, buttoning the crisp white blouse up to her neck and brushing the wrinkles out of her skirt. She had passed the exam that enabled her to be admitted to the Hengoed Girls' County School. Her parents had scrimped and saved just to be able to purchase her satchel and books. Bethan didn't take the honor of a grammar school education for granted. She worked hard on her lessons, seeking to make her parents proud of her.

Dressed for school, she felt her stomach growl. Driven by the irresistible call of hunger, she hastened down the narrow stairway.

Bethan's home was small, worn out, and right on the edge of ruin. But her mother did her best to keep it clean, and her father did his best to keep it repaired. Amidst the apparent challenges, love served as the binding glue that held it all together.

Bethan hurried down the short hallway and turned into the kitchen. "Breakfast smells wonderful, Mam," she said.

"Well, good morning, Bethan. I wasn't sure if you were ever going to get up," her mother, Catrin, said as she flipped the patty of laverbread she was frying. "Grab a plate and I will serve you. Bacon and tomatoes are on the table."

A staple of poor Welsh families, laverbread was made from seaweed. Often it was dried and then reconstituted into a paste, or mixed with oats to make a patty that was then fried.

Bethan's mother limped over to the table to serve her daughter the laverbread patties. A victim of childhood polio, the mother needed leg braces to walk. But she rarely slowed down as she worked to care for her little family.

While Bethan ate her breakfast, she heard the neighborhood children laughing and chattering as they walked past her house enroute to school. She gulped down the last of her meal, kissed her mother goodbye and dashed out the door to catch up to her friends.

Most of the children in Hengoed were born to poor collier families. All their fathers and their older brothers worked at the Penallta coal mine just outside of town. It was one of the largest mines in all of Wales. The mine had been producing coal since its founding in 1905 by the mine's owner, Powell Duffryn. What started as a small private mine that employed just 291 men had grown into a huge operation. In 1930, it employed more than 3,200 men and boys who proudly pulled a record 975,603 tons of coal out of the ground in just one year. Everyone in the town of Hengoed was benefited to some degree by the production of coal at the Penallta colliery.

Bethan and the other children knew nothing more than a life centered around the mine. As they skipped and giggled their way to school, no one paid any mind to the black curtain of smoke that hung in the air to the north of town. That was just the way things were in Hengoed.

A few streets away, Bethan turned to the left while the rest of the children on her street continued straight. The other children in her neighborhood attended the local government-run public school.

Bethan's father, Thomas, was a haulier. He worked with the pit ponies to pull the trams full of coal from the face of the coal seam to the pit head. Sending Bethan to the Hengoed Girls' Grammar School was quite a sacrifice for Bethan's parents, but her father was determined to make it happen for his precocious daughter.

In the evenings, dinner conversations often centered around the ponies, both large and small, as her father described their personalities. Bethan could tell that he thought of them as his best friends. She listened with rapt attention, trying to imagine what the gentle beasts were like. She had rarely even seen them since they were all stabled underground. Her only contact with them was when the train brought in a new load of horses to be schooled in the tasks of hauling the trams full of coal. Once they learned their jobs, they were lowered into the mines in a cage. Most would never see the light of day again.

"Tad," Bethan said on one occasion, "I saw some new pit ponies coming in for the mine today. But they were big. I thought ponies were supposed to be small. Why do you call them 'pit ponies' if they're so big?"

"Ay, my little peach," her father answered, "we use 'pit ponies' as a term of endearment. Indeed, the pit ponies at the Penallta mine are large, usually a mix of Shire horses and Welsh Mountain ponies. Most of the horses I work with are around 15 hands. Even larger ones are kept above ground for the work needed there."

"Are there any little ponies working in the mines?" Bethan asked.

"Not at Penallta, but several mines up north use little ponies because their coal seams are smaller than ours."

On another day, Thomas shared a story with his wife and daughter. "You should have seen what happened in the colliery today," he began. "I was just finishing harnessing Kit when I heard loud hoofbeats echoing from one of the tunnels." He paused his narrative long enough to cough several times into his napkin. No one paid his coughing any mind—that's just the way things were in Hengoed. Finally, he continued. "Suddenly, one of the ponies burst forth from the darkness, his broken harness flying out behind him. The flapping straps were the cause of his fear. Horses don't like what they can't see!"

"Oh, the poor baby," said Bethan. "He must've been terrified!"

Her mother clucked her tongue. "Seems like they have a lot of hauliers who don't know what they're doin'," she said, placing a bowl of mashed potatoes on the table.

"I'm afraid that's true," said Thomas. "Many are just teenage boys."

"Well, what happened to the pony?" Bethan prodded.

"I jumped out in front of him, my arms spread wide," he said, demonstrating his actions with his arms splaying to either side and waving up and down. "My antics spooked him enough to get him to turn into the stable."

"And the haulier? What happened to him?" asked Catrin.

"He came shufflin' back, cap in hand, face flushed with embarrassment, to the teasing of the other men."

"Well, I should think so," said Catrin.

"Tad, can you take me to see the pit ponies someday?" Bethan asked, patting his hand and giving him a loving smile.

"That's not likely, my little peach. The mines are no place for a young girl," her father said, grasping her hand in return. "You keep working on your studies and you'll be able to get a job more suited for a lady."

Catrin scoffed. "Thomas, I know of many mines that hire women and even girls."

"That may be true, Catrin," Thomas said, "and there may come a time when the Penallta colliery does the same. But I believe the work to be much too hard for a delicate woman. No wife or daughter of mine shall ever be a part of it. That's why I'm working so hard to send Bethan to that fancy school."

But life can take its unexpected twists and turns.

Chapter 3

Hengoed a few days later

The sun was dipping lower in the western sky, casting a golden hue over the landscape and the village storefronts. The fallen leaves were tossed in the air by a crisp breeze. Bethan reached out to catch a floating leaf as she walked home from school. She smiled as she examined the red and yellow colors mottled across its surface.

It had been a good day. She had done well on her assignments, even in math, which had been challenging for her up until this year. She started skipping, eager to get home and tell her mother about her success.

As she approached the cottage, she noticed her father waiting in the front yard. He was never expected home until nearly five in the evening, when his eight-to ten-hour shift at the mine ended. Her heart started racing. A cascade of thoughts surged through her mind. *What's wrong? Is Mam alright?* She broke into a run.

"Tad! Is something wrong?" she gasped.

"Bethan," her father replied, offering a reassuring smile. "All is well. I have something to show you, something that I believe will excite you. Follow me." Thomas took her hand and led her around the house to the backyard. Standing in a makeshift paddock was a shaggy, brown-and-white horse. His head was drooping, his long, thick forelock falling over his eyes.

Bethan jerked her hand away and covered her mouth. "Oh, my goodness. A pit pony. A real live pit pony! How? . . . Why? . . ."

Her father chuckled. "I knew you'd be excited. The poor fellow is here to recuperate. He's lame. The vet said he has an abscess in his hoof."

"Oh, the poor baby. Can I help you take care of him?"

"I'm expecting you to. His hoof needs to be treated three times a day. Do you think you can do that if I teach you how to doctor it?"

Bethan looked up at her father, determination in her eyes. Puffing out her chest and lifting her chin, she said, "I can, Tad. I will take excellent care of him."

"I knew you were just the one to do it," Thomas said, playfully ruffling her light-brown curls.

Bethan approached the fence. A thought suddenly occurred to her. Stopping abruptly, she turned to her father. "What do I call him? He must have a name, after all."

"Of course. All the pit ponies have a name. We call him Bryn."

Bethan squinted her eyes in thought. "Bryn? That means hill. Isn't that a bit of an odd name for a horse?"

"Not at all," Thomas said. "In fact, it's perfect." Swinging his arms in a wide circle at the surrounding landscape, he added, "What could be a better name for a horse whose work is creating these hills of coal slag all around us?"

◆ ◆ ◆ ◆ ◆ ◆ ◆ ◆ ◆ ◆

Bethan and her father immediately began treating Bryn's infected hoof. They made a healing poultice from peat moss and tore off strips of cotton fabric from an old rag Catrin provided. Leveraging Thomas's seasoned expertise in equine care, her father taught Bethan how to pick up the hoof and clean it. With practiced hands, he showed her how to spread the poultice over the sole with a wooden spatula. He guided her in placing the strips of cotton over and around the hoof to keep the poultice in place.

When at last Bryn's hoof was lowered to the ground, both stepped back and took a moment to admire their efforts. Thomas turned to Bethan, a glimmer of hope in his eyes. "Do you think you can do that on your own while I am at work?"

Bethan responded with a confident smile. "I can. I'm sure of it."

"Good. If we can nurse him back to health, we will save his life."

Bethan's eyes opened wide as the gravity of the situation sunk in. "What if I can't heal him?" Her voice quivered as the confidence she felt just moments before vanished.

Thomas dropped his chin and shook his head. "The mine owner has no need of a lame horse."

◆ ◆ ◆ ◆ ◆ ◆ ◆ ◆ ◆ ◆

For the next few weeks, Bethan rose before the sun, and in the gray dawn of each early morning, she set about doctoring Bryn's hoof. On school days, she ran home during lunchtime to do it again. Each evening, she treated it a third time, this session under the approving eye of her father.

After each treatment, she curried and brushed the horse until his long coat glistened. As she brushed, she sang a lullaby.

Close your eyes, little one,
'neath the Welsh moon's gentle glow,
In the meadow where the ponies softly
wander to and fro.

Hush now, dear child,
let the night breeze gently sigh,
As the stars above tell tales of ponies trotting by.

And as each day passed, Bethan's mother observed that her stock of apples and carrots, carefully cultivated from her garden, was depleting more rapidly than usual.

Chapter 4

Hengoed, fall 1937

Over the next two years, Thomas brought home many more pit ponies that needed special attention. Each one he brought home bore the scars of a life spent toiling in the dark depths of the earth.

Most arrived with coats matted with coal dust. Many were massive beasts, their powerful frames a testament to years of labor pulling heavy trams filled with coal.

The ponies he brought home came in a kaleidoscope of colors, from sleek blacks and bays to imposing greys. Most were geldings. Yet regardless of color or size, all needed some special care as their ailments mirrored the diversity of their appearances.

Some were valiantly fighting for their lives with such dangerous conditions as colic, their weakened bodies wracked with pain. Others bore the marks of their hazardous environment—deep cuts from unforgiving equipment that needed stitches and a clean environment that the mines could not provide. The mines also bred a sinister affliction known as "grease heel." Because of the damp conditions in which they worked, many horses developed painful swelling in their lower legs. The skin became raw, and the sores oozed with pus.

Recognizing the pressing need for attentive care, the company veterinarian soon discovered that Thomas and his daughter could provide the quality of care he didn't have the time to offer. This was a valuable service to both the horses and the owner of the mine.

Thus, in a world where time was precious and profit reigned supreme, Thomas and Bethan's selfless actions became a lifeline for both the horses and the mine owners. Their ability to deliver quality care where it was sorely needed not only alleviated the suffering of the pit ponies, but also safeguarded the profitability of the mines themselves.

For Bethan, life had magically become much more fulfilling. The simple act of being in the company of horses infused her young heart with a joy heretofore unknown. In tending to their well-being, Bethan unleashed a fresh and significant purpose that breathed vitality into her existence. And with each new patient, Bethan could tell she was falling in love—in love with both the horses and the job of caring for them.

♦ ♦ ♦ ♦ ♦ ♦ ♦ ♦ ♦ ♦

On her eleventh birthday, Bethan timidly approached her father who was comfortably settled in his well-worn chair by the crackling fire. Sundays marked his sole respite from the demanding toil of the mine. After returning from church services, he cherished a well-deserved break from the strenuous physical labor that defined the rest of his week. Bethan hesitated to even disturb him. But this was important.

"Tad?" she said, delicately breaking the silence.

Her father looked up from the book he was reading and coughed a few times before responding. "Yes, my little peach."

"Today is my birthday," she announced, a smile lighting up her face.

"Why, indeed it is," Thomas said, setting aside his book. "And how old might you be this day?" he asked, eyes twinkling.

"I'm eleven years old."

"Is that a fact? You are becoming quite a young lady. And what shall we do to celebrate?"

Bethan twisted her hands, then rubbed them nervously on her skirt. "I ... I ... "

"Out with it, child. I can see you have something on your mind."

"I would like to ride the pony."

Her father raised his eyebrows in surprise. "Ride the pony? Is that your birthday wish?"

"Dobbin is recovering well from his cut. All I wish is to amble around while perched on his back. It won't cause him any harm," she said earnestly.

◆ ◆ ◆ ◆ ◆ ◆ ◆ ◆ ◆

Thomas and Bethan walked out to the backyard where a bay horse stood in the paddock, watching them approach.

"Dobbin," Bethan called.

The gelding's ears twitched back and forth, and with a graceful toss of his large head, he stepped up to the fence.

"See, Tad. He likes me," Bethan said, gently caressing the gelding's forehead beneath his forelock.

"That he does." Thomas stepped through the gate and up to the gelding. Rubbing his neck, he added, "Dobbin has been my partner in the mines for nearly a year now. A steadier, more reliable horse I have yet to come across."

"You never told me how he got that terrible cut on his hip," Bethan said.

"One of the chains that we attach to the trams snapped and struck him."

"Oh, the poor baby. That must have been painful."

"I have no doubt of that. But you have done a wonderful job of taking care of the wound. There is no sign of infection, and it is nearly healed."

Bethan beamed with pride. "Thank you, Tad."

Then her father added something that tugged at her heart.

"I think I'll be able to return him to work next week."

Thomas noticed the melancholy look on Bethan's face. He lifted her chin with his work-roughened hand and looked into her eyes. "Oh, my little peach, don't look so sad. Dobbin has a job to do, just as all the men in the mine have. But let's not talk of work today. It's your birthday and you want to ride him. I can't think of a better present for an eleven-year-old."

Bethan's delighted squeal filled the air when her father reached down and scooped her up in the air. Dobbin turned his head and watched as the father gently placed his daughter on the gelding's broad back. Dobbin didn't move a muscle. "Go on," Thomas commanded as he started walking around the fence line. Dobbin, ever faithful to his trusted master, followed obediently.

Without a saddle to secure her seat and no bridle with which to guide, Bethan clutched Dobbin's thick mane with both hands, gripped his wide barrel with her legs, and let her body move naturally with the horse's movements.

"Oh, Tad, this is so much fun," she giggled. "I can't believe I'm actually riding a horse!"

Thomas turned and smiled at his daughter. As he did so, he gave Dobbin a rub on his neck, and the gelding nudged his muzzle against Thomas's arm.

Chapter 5

Hengoed, winter 1938

By the middle of winter, Dobbin had already been back at work in the Penallta Colliery for a few months, his injury healed nicely.

Six days a week, Thomas entered the large cage awaiting him at the top of the pit, accompanied by several other men and boys. The cage descended over two thousand feet, transporting the miners to the pit floor. Once at the bottom, Thomas and the other men walked down one of the two tunnels to their assigned jobs. Thomas, as a haulier, walked a short distance to the underground stable. Typically, the stables were constructed early in any colliery's life. They were usually located quite close to the pit bottom. Such strategic positioning helped channel the unpleasant odor emanating from the stables up and out the mine shaft, preventing it from permeating through the tunnels.

Arriving at the stables, Thomas breathed in the heady scent of leather, hay, and manure—an aroma that to some might be unpleasant, but which brought a smile to Thomas' face. His first task was to make sure the men in charge of caring for the horses during the night had done a good job by giving Dobbin clean, fresh feed and cleaning his stall. Thomas gave the horse a good grooming before putting on the harness that would connect him to the tram. It was a routine both had come to expect and enjoy.

Before he led Dobbin to the empty tram, he put leather headgear on the horse that protected his head and eyes. If they were working at a seam that didn't have lanterns or electric lights, Thomas used a pressed cardboard helmet that had an oil lamp attached to it. He generally walked in front of Dobbin so the horse could see ahead into the tunnel.

The last piece of equipment that Thomas placed on Dobbin was a leather pad over the croup, the high point of his hind quarters. If this pad were to get a scrape on it from trying to pass through a tunnel that was too low, the miners knew they would have to cut out more of the floor to give the horse room to pass.

The tunnels in the Penallta mine had rails on which the trams rolled. This made it easier for the horses to pull a fully loaded tram. But the ground between the rails was often rough and rocky. The pit ponies had to pick their way through the dark tunnels so as not to stumble and fall. Because of the hard, uneven ground, the last safety check Bethan's father always did was to examine each hoof to make sure the steel shoes were secure. Overly worn shoes with risen clenches, the nails that secured the shoe to the wall of the hoof, could come off in the tunnels and cause damage to the hoof. The old saying, "No hoof, no horse," certainly applied to the pit ponies in the coal mining tunnels of Wales.

Grooming and tacking-up complete, Thomas smiled and said, "Are ye going to work for me today?' Dobbin gave a toss of his head and was rewarded with a slice of apple.

At the end of the long day, Thomas led Dobbin back to the stable, removed his harness, and washed the black coal dust off the gelding's long coat. Thomas led him to his stall, clearly marked with Dobbin's name carved on a wooden plaque, and made sure the horse had a generous helping of oats and a manger full of hay.

"It's been a good day, today, my friend," he said as he rubbed Dobbin's neck. "Have a good rest for tomorrow is the Sabbath."

◆ ◆ ◆ ◆ ◆ ◆ ◆ ◆ ◆

One particularly cold and windy day, Thomas sloshed through the mud on his way to the mine. The falling rain was being blown before the breeze. He walked with his head down, letting his cap shield his face from the sputtering rain. He didn't acknowledge any of the other men also making their way to work the early shift at the mine, though they were all walking along the same route. Nor did any of the men pay him any mind. The frequent sound of coughing was the only indication that they were even there. Yet there was an unspoken understanding that they were all in this together. You worked, you slept, you worked again. That's just the way things were in Hengoed.

At this time of day, the sun had not yet made its appearance, but he knew his way through the dark streets. The light of day was something he witnessed only on the Sabbath or during the long days of summer. He chuckled to himself as he realized he was looking forward to the shelter the mine provided. Though the lighting in the mine was dim—electric lights were just starting to be used and currently only in the stables—the tunnels at least offered protection from the wind and cold. Many men even shed their shirts while chipping away at the wall of coal.

Thomas chose to walk to the mine rather than take the small local bus some of the men used. He needed to save every shilling to pay for Bethan's school. He was proud of his daughter for qualifying to be admitted to the private girls' school. He had dreams for his only child, dreams that did not include a life in the mines. With a good education, Bethan could become a nurse, or a teacher, or work in one of the large offices in Cardiff.

Thomas had just finished hooking Dobbin to the empty tram when he heard a horse's high-pitched squeal, followed by a loud crash echoing down the stone walls of one of the tunnels. He jerked up from where he was bending over behind Dobbin. Suddenly, the horse's squeals were joined by the angry shouts of a man and the sound of banging on metal.

Thomas left Dobbin and started running toward the sound.

"Dang horse," a man was yelling. "I said turn right!" The horse responded by bucking within the shafts to which he was harnessed and kicking back at the tram. This was met with more yelling and cursing.

Thomas ran up to the man and grabbed his raised arm before he could hit the horse with the sprag, a piece of round timber with sharpened ends that was usually used to place in a tram wheel as a brake.

"Stop! That's no way to treat yer pony," he said, anger causing blood to rush to his face.

"What ya doin', man?" the haulier growled. "Let go 'o me arm!"

Thomas noticed the haulier was just a young lad, probably not more than fifteen. No doubt he was inexperienced with horses. Thomas took a deep breath to calm himself, his hand still gripping the arm of the boy.

"I'll let go when ye drop the sprag," Thomas said.

"Well, how am I supposed to get the beast to move if I don't hit him?"

Thomas looked the boy in the eye and his thoughts went back to his early days in the mine when he had first been assigned to be a haulier. At that time, he had much to learn and had been taken under the wing of an old miner with decades of experience. He was grateful for what his mentor taught him before the old man's lung ailment forced him to retire.

"Yer givin' him the wrong commands," Thomas said, speaking slowly and keeping his voice soft.

"What do ye mean? What should I be sayin'?"

"He's been taught to respond to verbal commands. If ye want him to turn right, ye say 'Gun on.' If ye want him to turn left, say 'Come here.' Turn around? Say 'Come here back.' Walk backwards? Say 'Come back.' He'll do the right thing if he knows what ye want."

The boy's mouth twisted, and his eyes squinted skeptically. "Horses ain't that smart."

"Oh, aren't they?" Thomas said. "Let's just see about that." Standing behind the tram, in a voice that was both firm and kind, Thomas said, "Gun on."

The horse's ears twitched and he turned his head slightly. Then he lowered his neck and pushed his shoulders into the harness. The tram started rolling and he turned to the right, down a narrow, dark tunnel.

The boy remained frozen in place, his mouth hanging open as he stared at the back of the tram. "I don't believe it" He looked over at Thomas, dropped his chin, and rubbed the back of his neck. "I guess I have a lot to learn to be a haulier."

Thomas gave him a comforting pat on the shoulder. "Learning takes time, but always keep in mind that, just like people, horses respond more positively to kindness than cruelty." Thomas chuckled as he gave the lad a gentle shove forward. "I guess you had better catch up with yer horse."

Chapter 6

Penallta Colliery in South Wales, spring 1938

Bethan missed Dobbin and made sure that her father brought the gelding a daily apple or carrot from their pantry. Her mother worried they would run out of carrots before they ran out of winter. But she turned her back and kept her mouth shut.

Each day after school, Bethan hurried home, hoping a new pit pony had arrived for her to nurse back to health. She was always disappointed each day their little paddock was empty.

One bright spring day, as the village children bent over their school desks working on their math problems, the dreaded sound of a steam whistle filled the air. Work at the mine was being stopped, which meant something was wrong. All the children jerked their heads up, their eyes wide with worry.

At Hengoed Girls' County School, the teacher tried to comfort her students. "Yes, young ladies. There seems to have been an accident at the mine. It may be nothing serious at all, so try not to worry too much. Let's put our books away and finish our assignments tomorrow so you can go home and be with your families. I'm sure we'll find out soon what the problem is."

The girls didn't need any more encouragement, and the room was soon empty. The children from both the grammar school and the public school ran to their respective cottages to await the news from the mine.

Bethan dashed out the entrance of the Hengoed Girls' County School, allowing the door to bang shut behind her. Sprinting homeward, her arms strained under the weight of the satchel. Her long, wavy locks billowed out behind her.

She arrived home to find her mother pacing back and forth in the front yard. Her eyes were fixed on the black smoke coming from the direction of the mine. A sense of unease permeated the neighborhood. Several other neighbors were in their yards as well, some in clusters wearing anxious looks and chatting quietly; others, like her mother, worrying in silence and solitude.

Bethan ran up to her mother. "Mam, what's happening?"

Her mother took her hand and squeezed it tightly. "It appears there has been an accident at the mine."

Bethan heard the tremor in her mother's voice and saw the worry etched across her face. "Is Tad alright?"

Mam knelt in front of Bethan and enveloped her in her arms. "We haven't heard anything. All we can do is wait and pray."

◆ ◆ ◆ ◆ ◆ ◆ ◆ ◆ ◆ ◆

Earlier in the day, several hours before the steam whistle alerted the town to danger in the mine, Thomas and Dobbin were going about their usual routine. With practiced precision, they navigated the narrow passageways, their footsteps echoing off the damp walls. They hauled an empty tram to the coal seam where a loaded tram was awaiting them. The area was called a "tumble up" in that it was a space cut out of the side of the roadway that was wide enough for the miners to set the empty tram while the pit pony pulled the full tram away. The maneuver was quite difficult.

With little more than a brief greeting to his fellow miners, Thomas secured the empty tram in place using the sprag to block the wheels. Dobbin stood patiently as his master unhitched the shaft from the front of the tram. Then, at Thomas' command,

Dobbin pivoted his body one hundred and eighty degrees away from the empty tram so two miners could remove, or "tumble" that tram off the track. Even empty, this was an extremely challenging task as the trams were made of steel and quite heavy. With grunts of effort and faces etched with determination, the men wrested the cumbersome steel box from its tracks, their muscles straining against the weight. The tram creaked in protest as it was moved off the rails, the metal clang reverberating through the cavernous chamber.

With the empty tram out of the way, Thomas hitched Dobbin to the fully loaded tram and got ready to head back to the pit opening. Dobbin lowered his head, squeezed his eyes shut, and pushed hard against the leather collar of the harness, trying to get the tram rolling. The metal wheels screeched as they scraped against the rails. They slowly started turning. Dobbin dug his hooves deeper into the ground and groaned. The wheels made a scratching sound as they turned a little more. With a final burst of strength, Dobbin had the tram moving.

The hike back to the pit mouth was over a mile and took nearly an hour to complete. By the time they reached the opening, Dobbin's coat was wet with sweat and coated with coal dust. Thomas unhitched the tram so it could be hauled to the surface by the windlass, a winding gin powered by two horses on the surface. Thomas watched with both relief and a touch of pride as the full tram was lifted out of the mine.

Satisfied that they had completed the task at hand, Thomas and Dobbin took a lunch break, what they called a "bait-stand," before starting back to the coal face with an empty tram to repeat the difficult process. Dobbin took a long drink of water from the trough and nibbled some grain from the feed bag Thomas secured to his headstall.

Thomas sat on the hitching plate of the tram and ate his lunch of bread and cheese, slowly savoring each bite. He quenched his thirst by taking refreshing sips of water from a tin bottle. Bait-stand never seemed to last long enough. Such was life in the coal mine.

"Rest time is over, old boy," Thomas said as he removed the feed bag and rubbed the white stripe that cascaded down the center of Dobbin's face.

An empty tram made going deep into the mine much easier, and in no time at all, they were halfway to the face. Suddenly, Dobbin jerked his head up, ears twitching, and stopped.

Lost in his own thoughts, Thomas didn't notice when the hoofbeats and the scraping sound from the wheels on the rails stopped.

Dobbin whinnied.

This caught Thomas' attention and he turned back. "Dobbin? What's the matter?"

Dobbin snorted and pawed the ground.

"Dobbin? What is it?"

Dobbin began backing away and, in that moment, Thomas discerned the unmistakable sound of rocks crashing against one another as they started falling. His heart quickened, propelling him to sprint back toward Dobbin as he desperately yelled the command to back up. "Come back! Come back!"

But it was too late. A large section of the roof above Thomas fell in a thunderous crash, hurling him forward onto his stomach and trapping his legs.

Dobbin stopped in mid-stride. He whinnied, the sound echoing down the dark stone tunnel. But Thomas didn't answer. Silence filled the mine and Dobbin seemed to know instinctively that the threat was over, at least for the moment. He lowered his head and walked forward. Reaching his master where he lay on the rocky ground, Dobbin pulled off Thomas' cap and ruffled his hair with his top lip.

Thomas groaned and brushed the horse away. Dobbin licked Thomas' face. Thomas opened his eyes and wiped his cheek. Looking up at Dobbin, he grimaced. "I need . . . your . . . help, old b-boy," he whispered between clenched teeth.

Thomas reached up with both hands and took hold of Dobbin's headstall. "Come back!" he commanded. Keeping his head down, the pit pony pulled Thomas' injured body out from under the pile of rocks that was pinning his legs.

Thomas cried out in pain. Dobbin's ears twitched back and forth. Thomas hooked his arms more securely through the headstall, closed his eyes, and choked out the command one final time: "Come back!"

Chapter 7

The sun was just setting when the news of the collapse at the mine reached the waiting families in Hengoed. Two miners were trapped at the end of one tunnel and had to be dug out. Their happy families were relieved to see them walking out, covered in black coal dust but unhurt.

Thomas, however, having been dragged away from the cave-in toward the pit by Dobbin, was in quite rough shape. Both of his legs were broken by the falling rocks, and cuts and abrasions covered his lower body from being dragged over the rough ground. His clothing was shredded. When Dobbin was found backing down the track by the men who had been sent to rescue their mates, they discovered an unconscious Thomas hanging from the horse's harness. But, thanks to his pit pony, Thomas was alive.

Thomas was taken directly to the hospital. A miner was sent to fetch his wife and daughter.

♦ ♦ ♦ ♦ ♦ ♦ ♦ ♦ ♦ ♦

For several days, Thomas lay in a coma, his wife faithfully remaining by his side. The staff at the hospital continued to reassure her that they were doing all they could to save his life. Both legs had been set in casts in hopes that the broken bones would heal.

On the fourth day, Thomas opened his eyes. He struggled to focus on the dim light in the strange room. Unfamiliar sounds—voices, and machines beeping—caused him to try to sit up. Grasping the side of the bed, he found he couldn't move. He looked around and noticed his wife asleep in a chair beside the bed he found himself in.

"Catrin," he whispered, his throat parched and aching.

Awakening abruptly, his wife gasped. "Thomas. Oh, Thomas," she said, tears welling in her eyes and coursing down her cheeks. She reached for his outstretched hand.

♦ ♦ ♦ ♦ ♦ ♦ ♦ ♦ ♦ ♦

While Thomas recovered, the mining families gathered around Bethan and her mother, offering support by way of meals and help around the house. But both Catrin and Thomas knew they could not rely on others for long. Their neighbors were poor families, struggling to support their own.

"What are we going to do?" Catrin sighed, dropping her chin to her chest. "The rent will be due soon and without your paycheck, our meager savings will soon disappear."

Thomas stared at the ceiling of the hospital room. The sound of his familiar coughing filled the room. Catching his breath, he said, "I don't know, my love. I just don't know. I promise I'll get back to work as soon as I am able."

"I know you will, my darling. But that could be several months yet."

◆ ◆ ◆ ◆ ◆ ◆ ◆ ◆ ◆ ◆

The next day, Bethan accompanied her mother to her father's bedside. Her mother stood behind her, hands on her daughter's shoulders.

Bethan smiled as she took her father's hand. "Tad, you look better today."

"Do I? That's good to hear," he said, forcing himself to return the smile. "And what has my little peach been up to? How is school going?"

"It has been going quite well. I love it," Bethan said. She looked over her shoulder at her mother before continuing. "But, Tad, there is something I need to tell you."

"What's that?" Thomas said. "And what could it be that causes such a sad face on my little girl?"

"I . . . I withdrew from school today, Tad," she said. She pursed her lips to try to stop them from quivering. She turned her head to one side and blinked away a tear.

"What?" shouted Tad, as he tried to sit up with little success. "You did what?" he repeated just as loudly.

"Thomas, lay back down and listen to what we have decided," Catrin said.

"We? I don't believe I was included in any decisions. I have worked so hard to enable our daughter to go to that fancy school. And now you tell me she is withdrawing?" He pounded his fist on the bed. "I don't believe this! I won't have it!"

"It's only for a short time, Thomas," Catrin said. "Just until you are better and can start working again. But Bethan and I need to take over providing for the family while you recover."

Thomas flopped back on his pillow and groaned. His eyes narrowed and his mouth dropped into a deep frown. "And just what have the two of you decided to do?"

"I am going to take in laundry," Catrin said.

Thomas nodded as he looked down at the braces that covered her legs. "Do you think you are strong enough to do that?"

"Of course, I am," she answered confidently.

Looking over at Bethan, Thomas said, "And what are you planning to do that will take you away from school?"

"I'm going to go to work in the mine, Tad," Bethan said, lifting her chin and staring into his eyes.

"No! I forbid it," Thomas said as he again struggled to sit up. "It's much too dangerous."

"Tad, I can do this. There are several jobs for children at the mine. I won't even have to go underground. I can work on the sorting tables."

"You have no idea what you would be getting into. The work is too hard for a little girl," Thomas moaned, covering his face in his hands.

"I'm not a little girl. I'm eleven and a half."

Thomas shook his head. "Even if you stay on the surface, you'll be around a lot of rough men and boys. That is not an environment I want my little girl in."

Thomas lowered his hands to his sides and clutched the bed linens as the family meeting dragged painfully on. He looked away, his jaw twitching.

Catrin sat on the edge of her husband's bed. "We have looked into other options. The mine is the only place that will give her a job."

"But her schooling . . ." Thomas said, lying back down and running his hands through his wavy, brown hair. "Why? Oh, why did this have to happen?"

Bethan leaned forward and gave her father a hug. "It's okay. I can get back to school when you are healed."

Catrin clasped one of his hands. "We will get through this together. Your only job is to heal. Don't worry about us."

Thomas turned his face away, not wanting his family to see his tears.

Chapter 8

Hengoed, spring 1938

ethan endured a restless night as her once-comfortable world crumbled around her. The life she cherished was disappearing. Having to leave school broke *her* heart as much as it did her father's. Yet she didn't hesitate. Her father needed her help, and she would be there for him just as he had always been for her.

The prospect of toiling in the mine, even if not underground, filled her with dread. Observing the miners trudge home at the end of the day, their shoulders slouching, their faces and clothing covered in black coal dust, vividly conveyed the arduous nature of their labor. Thoughts swirled in her head:

Would she be able to carry her load? Would the miners be kind to her?

Seeking solace, she burrowed down beneath her coverlet and squeezed her eyes shut. Eventually, sleep triumphed over her lingering apprehension.

Bethan was awakened by her mother the next morning, well before the sun made its appearance. "Bethan, it's time to wake up," she said tenderly. "I have clothing for you, a gift from the neighbor's son who has outgrown them."

Bethan sat up, suddenly wide awake. "Boy's clothes?" she said, her brow knitted.

"I realize it isn't proper, but I think they will hold up better, especially the boots. I also think it will be safer. I wouldn't want your petticoats to get caught in the gears and chains."

Bethan dropped her chin. "Yes, Mam." She put on the shirt made from fine sacking and buttoned it to her neck. She placed the wool vest over the top. The red worsted stockings came next followed by the brown flannel trousers. Finally, she slipped her feet into the heavy boots, reinforced with hobnails and toecaps, and laced them tightly.

After Bethan dressed, her mother tied her hair up in a knot and placed it inside a woolen cap. "To keep your lovely locks clean," she said. Satisfied with her work, she added, "There! Would you like to look at yourself in the mirror?"

Bethan approached the vintage mirror in the hallway and was taken aback. For all eleven years of her life, she had worn long dresses and petticoats. Her hair flowed over her shoulders in light-brown waves or thick braids. As she stood before the mirror, the reflection staring back at her was of someone she didn't know. "Oh, Mam," she exclaimed, tears welling up and bursting forth.

Her mother hurried over and embraced her quivering body. "It will be fine. The neighbors will watch out for you. And it's just for a short time. You'll be back in school soon."

Bethan ate her breakfast in silence, her mind awash in anxiety and doubt. A profound sigh escaped her as she gently pushed her plate away and rose from her seat. "I suppose it's time," she said as she lifted her chin.

As Bethan headed for the door, Catrin handed her daughter a tin box. Bethan recognized it as her father's choppy-box. "Here's your lunch," Catrin said. "Don't eat it all at once as it will have to last the entire day. Oh, and don't let the rats get to it."

Bethan's eyes opened wide. "Rats?"

Catrin frowned as she nodded. Reaching out, she took her young daughter in her arms. "I'm so sorry you are having to do this. But I want you to know how much Tad and I appreciate it."

Bethan walked through the misty darkness to the Penallta mine. She was not alone on the road as other men and boys, saving their shillings by not taking the bus, walked the same route. Very little chatter was exchanged between coworkers, and no one spoke to her. Bethan hugged herself and kept her eyes down. She felt her throat thicken and her eyes start to sting. The world had never seemed so dark and lonely.

The large black buildings of the Penallta mine loomed ahead. The smokestacks reached into the grey sky like sentinels. A few newly installed electric lights sparkled like beacons in the early dawn, offering just the tiniest bit of comfort. She followed the others as they entered the main building.

A boy who appeared to be her age approached from one side. "Ye a new lad here?" he said.

Bethan turned in surprise, her large hazel eyes widening. "Pardon me?"

The boy stopped in shock. "Ye not be a lad?"

Bethan dropped her chin and shook her head.

"I not seen a tip girl at this mine before."

Bethan recognized the name used for girls who worked in the coal mines of South Wales. "It's my first day," she whispered, her words barely audible over the grinding of the machines echoing in the cavernous building. "I don't know where to go."

"Ah. Let me show ye to the manager's office. He'll give ye yer assignment."

Bethan managed a tight smile. "Thank you."

The boy led Bethan to one side of the large metal building and up to a black door. Pushing it open, he said, "Just go in here and get your work assignment from the man at the desk."

The office was a noisy place with men coming and going. Bethan was jostled through the crowd of large bodies until she found herself standing in front of a thick, wooden desk. Seated behind it was a slim man wearing round spectacles. She cleared her throat and said, "Sir, I'm here to work."

The man looked up and immediately his face softened. "Ah, Thomas's daughter. I've been expecting you. I hope your father is doing well?"

Bethan nodded.

"He was our best haulier. The pit ponies all loved him. I hope he'll be back with us soon."

"As do I," Bethan said meekly.

The man chuckled. "Yes, I'm sure you do." He shuffled through the papers on his desk. "Ah, here it is. Can you read and write?"

"Yes, sir."

"Good. Read this and sign at the bottom. Your pay is eight shillings a week. You will be paid at the end of the week."

Bethan looked up in surprise. "Eight shillings? My father was paid eleven shillings."

"Yes. He was a man doing man's work. You are but a child—and a girl, at that."

Bethan sighed, but she took the proffered pen and signed her name.

"Now, young lady, the Mines and Collieries Act of 1842 forbids women and girls from working underground, so you will be working in the sorting area. Your job will be to riddle the coal to separate it from the culm. Your shift will start at six a.m. and will usually last for eight hours, though sometimes as long as ten. You will be expected to work six days a week, with Sundays off." The man stood abruptly. "Follow me. I'll show you where to go."

The man was quite tall, making Bethan feel even smaller and less significant. Gathering her courage, she lifted her chin and followed him out of the office and across the large building. There, trams brimming with coal were being unloaded by the hands of boys both her age and older. Other boys were raking the coal, and still others were loading the sorted chunks of coal into new trams hitched to a horse.

The manager handed her a rake. "Here you go. Oh, and you can put your tin on that shelf over there. Don't feed the rats."

With that, he turned and left.

Chapter 9

Penallta Colliery, the first day

The work was harder than Bethan had imagined it would be. She pulled her metal rake across the chunks of coal, dragging them toward the edge of the pile, leaving the black dust behind. Over and over, she stretched the rake forward and pulled it back. By the time the bell rang for the bait-stand, her arms and shoulders ached, and her face was smeared with black coal dust from wiping the perspiration off her forehead. She looked down at her hands. Blisters were already forming.

She retrieved her choppy-box from the wooden shelf and sat down on a rusty, upturned bucket. Her mother had sent her cheese and bread and a tin of water. She leaned over to place her box on the ground.

"Don't put that on the ground."

Bethan started and looked up. The boy who had helped her earlier stood before her, a smile across his blackened face.

"You wouldn't want the rats to get it."

"Everyone keeps warning me about the rats," she said, closing the lid of her tin box.

"That's because they're everywhere."

"I haven't seen any."

"Watch this." With a mischievous grin, the boy broke off a piece of brown bread and tossed it toward a pile of equipment. Instantly, three large grey rats emerged from beneath the metal and began engaging in a lively skirmish, each determined to claim the bread for itself. Claws slashed as each emitted high-pitched squeaks and hisses. The largest of the rats soon dashed away from the chaos, the chunk of bread triumphantly carried in his mouth. The others followed, still hissing.

Bethan jerked back. "I see what you mean," she said, her voice quivering.

"May I sit here?" he asked, motioning toward an anvil sitting nearby.

"Please. I would love some company."

"I know what you mean. There isn't much time to talk to people once the work begins." The boy pulled out another chunk of bread from his choppy-box and took a bite. "My name is Dylan," he said between bites.

"I'm Bethan."

"Pleased to make yer acquaintance."

Bethan nodded and smiled.

"So, today is yer first day," he said. "I remember my first day as if it were only yesterday."

"And how long ago was it?" Bethan asked, stifling a chuckle.

"Over a year now. I'm thirteen already," he said, puffing up his chest.

"Oh. I see. I'm almost twelve. Actually, I'm only eleven and a half," she said, looking down to hide the blush on her cheeks.

"That's how old I was when I started working here," Dylan said before taking another bite of bread. He looked over at her choppy-box. "You might want to save some of that for later in the day."

Bethan snapped her box shut.

The afternoon was slightly more pleasant as Dylan took up riddling right beside her. Having him near made her feel less alone, even though they rarely spoke.

Near the end of the long day, Bethan felt her muscles start to tremble as the rake fell from her hands. She looked down. Her blisters had broken open and red streaks of blood covered the handle of the rake. She stopped, her head down, her arms hanging as though lifeless at her sides.

Dylan dropped his own rake and ran over to her. "Bethan, are ye okay?"

"I just can't do any more," she said with a whimper.

The sorting area supervisor who was working the trams as they came up from the pit hurried over to her. "You have been working hard today," he said, placing a gentle hand on her shoulder. "Better than most on their first day, I might add. Go home now. Tomorrow is the Sabbath. Get a good rest and come back on Monday."

"Thank you, sir," Bethan answered. "But I need to finish my shift."

"We are almost done for the day, anyway," the supervisor said. "Your father would be proud of how hard you have worked. And don't worry, it will get easier. I promise." He started to walk away, then turned back. "Dylan, why don't you walk her home. Just to make sure she makes it safely. And Bethan, have your mother treat those blisters."

"Thank you, sir. I will," Dylan said.

Chapter 10

Penallta Colliery, the end of the day and the
start of the next

Two exhausted children shuffled wearily down the road, leaving the black smokestacks behind. Every limb in Bethan's body ached; every muscle was spent. Her blisters stung. She felt that she could collapse at any moment and never get up.

With Bethan dressed in boys' clothing and covered in black coal dust, none of the neighborhood children, playing in their yards on their day off from school, recognized her—a fact that brought her a sense of relief. She didn't know how the other children would treat her now that she was a tip girl. Would they tease her or belittle her?

Throughout the day, there had been a hint of rain in the air. As Bethan and Dylan walked home it started to fall in great drops, sending the neighborhood children running for their homes. Bethan and Dylan were soon soaked to their skin, their faces covered in black streaks as the rain ran in tiny rivulets off their caps. Bethan shivered from both the cold and a fear she would never find her way home through the downpour.

Relying on Dylan, she forced herself to keep moving. At last, they reached her humble cottage.

Her mother threw the door wide open as they approached. "Bethan, are you ill?"

"Just very tired, Mam."

"She worked as well as any man," Dylan said. "You should be proud."

Catrin shifted her attention to Dylan. "Thank you for bringing her home, young man."

"This is my new friend, Dylan," Bethan managed to say before collapsing on the porch steps.

◆ ◆ ◆ ◆ ◆ ◆ ◆ ◆ ◆ ◆

After a restful Sunday, Monday arrived all too quickly. Bethan woke from a deep sleep with a heart weighed down by dread. Yet, her visit to her father's bedside the previous day ignited a renewed determination within her.

As she departed from her family's little cottage, she noticed Dylan waiting for her in the street. A warm feeling radiated through her chest, and the day didn't seem quite so dark anymore. She felt herself bouncing lightly as she walked toward him.

"Dylan," she said. "I'm so glad to see you."

"I thought I'd see if you were up to going to the mine today. I have quite a fun activity planned. It involves a rake and lots of coal."

Bethan could not contain a burst of laughter. "Yes. I think that's a splendid idea."

"I brought you something," he said, blushing.

Bethan cocked her head in surprise. "What?"

Dylan pulled a set of old work gloves from his pocket. "These are too small for me now. Besides, I don't need them anymore. My hands are tough now."

Bethan put the gloves on her bandaged hands and looked up at Dylan. "Thank you. They'll be perfect."

They walked through the darkness, chatting merrily. Bethan's heart brimmed with gratitude toward Dylan, recognizing the depth of his kindness. In that moment, she grasped the profound truth that confronting life's challenges becomes much easier with a friend at your side.

They had just found their spot in the sorting area when the manager of the mine approached. Bethan watched him, filled with trepidation. Had she done something wrong? Was she in trouble for leaving early on Saturday?

"Bethan and Dylan," he began, his voice gruff.

Bethan gripped her rake tightly.

Then his face softened. He pulled out two envelopes. "You left without collecting your pay."

Bethan felt tears of relief stinging her eyes. "Yes. Thank you," she whispered as she took the envelope and stuffed it in the pocket of her jacket.

"Now get to work," he said. "And try to make it the whole day, will you?"

"Yes, sir," Bethan and Dylan said in unison.

It could not have been even an hour later when the manager approached Bethan a second time. This time, she hadn't noticed him coming and the tap on her shoulder caused her to jump. She turned abruptly. Her eyes widened in surprise.

"Bethan, it seems the hauliers are having a bit of trouble with Dobbin."

Bethan's brow knitted. "Trouble?"

"It seems he refuses to work for anyone but your father."

"Oh no," she said, pushing her cap back from her forehead. "What are you going to do?"

"Let me just say the mine owner has no need of a horse that will not work."

Bethan looked down at the ground and tapped her rake. "I understand," she said softly.

"But I have an idea."

Bethan looked up; her eyes hopeful.

"I know you helped care for Dobbin when he was injured. Perhaps he would work for you. Perhaps you could be his haulier."

Bethan's jaw dropped as she let out a gasp. "Me? But I'm a girl. Doesn't the law forbid girls from working underground?"

"Dressed like that, you don't look like one to me," he said with a sly grin. Looking around, he added, "I don't think anyone here will tell, do you?"

Bethan's cheeks blushed beneath the layer of coal dust. "If you think I won't get in trouble, I would love to try."

"Good. Come with me."

Bethan glanced over at Dylan, who had been watching and listening to the exchange. With a slight lift of her hand, she waved. Dylan mirrored the gesture, his expression a blend of sadness and curiosity.

◆ ◆ ◆ ◆ ◆ ◆ ◆ ◆ ◆ ◆

A few minutes later, Bethan stepped into the metal cage that would lower her over two thousand feet to the base of the pit. Her heart was pounding, and her hands were cold and clammy as they gripped the mesh lining the sides of the cage. Her heart jumped to her throat as the cage started its descent.

With a jolt, the cart touched down at the pit's bottom. A robust man, a lamp affixed to his helmet, swung open the gate on the cage and greeted her. "Thomas' daughter? I didn't expect you to be so young."

"Yes, sir."

"I understand you have a way with Dobbin."

"I love him, sir."

"Yes, well, we love all the pit ponies in the mine when they do their jobs. We have no use for the ones who won't."

"I understand, sir," Bethan answered, before biting her lower lip.

"Good. So, you understand what we are up against." Handing her a helmet with a small oil light attached, he added, "I'm Morys. I'm the ostler here in the mine. It's my job to look after the horses and train the hauliers."

"Yes, sir," Bethan said as she lifted her chin and looked up to the distant opening in the earth from which she had been lowered. A wave of dizziness overcame her, and she grasped the side of the cage.

"We have a short walk to the stables. Follow me."

Bethan clenched her teeth and placed the helmet on her head. She hesitated but a moment, then started walking behind Morys into the dark unknown.

Chapter 11

The walls of the tunnel down which they walked were black stone and exuded an air of mystery and danger. Bethan walked between metal rails set in the ground on which the trams rolled. She often stumbled over the uneven ground and was grateful for the sturdy boots her neighbor had gifted her. At intervals, she walked beneath wooden rafters that had been erected, providing structural support to the subterranean path.

Bethan's senses were heightened as their footsteps reverberated off the tunnel walls. Amidst the darkness, the drip-drop of unseen water added an eerie enhancement to the rhythm of their steps. This was accompanied by the scurrying of rats, their presence only hinted at by the rustling in the shadows. *Rats,* she thought. *More rats!* A shiver ran down her spine.

They turned a corner and Bethan was relieved to see the glow from electric lights up ahead.

"We've just recently installed electric lights at the stable," Morys said, a touch of pride in his voice. "It makes working with the ponies much easier."

Arriving at the underground stables, Bethan was surprised at what she saw. A long row of standing stalls was constructed along a second tunnel built perpendicular to the main one. The stable was fifty or sixty yards long, ten feet wide and eight feet high. Each standing stall was constructed with whitewashed brick walls dividing the horses. A manger was built in the front. The back side was open to the aisleway. A pony's name was painted on a wooden plaque above each stall. Most of the stalls were currently empty.

Suddenly, Bethan heard stomping and kicking. A man began yelling and swearing from a stall far down the row. He jumped out into the aisleway. "Dang monster! I'll not work with him, I won't!" he growled, rubbing his right shoulder with his left hand.

"Dobbin is at it again," said Morys. He looked down at Bethan. "I hope you can do something with him, or he will have to go."

Bethan felt her stomach twist. "I'll try, sir."

She walked down the aisle between the tracks, passing stalls on her right and a big room on the left labeled "Choppy House" where the feed was kept. As she walked, she started singing her lullaby.

Close your eyes little one,
'neath the Welsh moon's gentle glow,
In the meadow where the ponies
softly wander to and fro.
Hush now, dear child,
let the night breeze gently sigh,
As the stars above tell tales of ponies trotting by.

The stomping and kicking stopped as Bethan's young, sweet voice carried down the stable, amplified by the stone walls.

Arriving at the stall labeled "Dobbin," she sang again.

Close your eyes, little one,
'neath the Welsh moon's gentle glow,
In the meadow where the ponies
softly wander to and fro.
Hush now, dear child,
let the night breeze gently sigh,
As the stars above tell tales of ponies trotting by.

Dobbin turned his head. His large, brown eyes, now warm and gentle, stared at her. He nickered softly.

"Oh, Dobbin," Bethan said as she stepped into his stall.

"Wait, child, you better not . . ." the miner who had been driven out earlier started to warn.

But it was too late. Bethan was at Dobbin's head, her face buried in his shaggy mane.

◆ ◆ ◆ ◆ ◆ ◆ ◆ ◆ ◆ ◆

The rest of the morning was spent teaching Bethan how to harness Dobbin, including placing the headgear with eye shields over his head for protection. Straps seemed to go every which way in a confusing maze across his body.

When Morys was satisfied that Bethan could handle the harness, he let her lead Dobbin out of his stall and between the tram rails toward the main tunnel. Here he taught her how to attach the harness to the tram. Dobbin stood patiently.

The final step, and the most difficult, was learning how to drive or lead Dobbin through the tunnel as he pulled the tram. Just as Thomas had taught the other new boys, Morys taught Bethan the verbal commands. "If ye want him to go forward, say 'Go on'. If you want him to turn right, you say 'Gun on.' Turn left? Say 'Come here.' Turn around? Say 'Come here back.' Walk backwards? Say 'Come back.'"

"Light your headlamp here at the stable before you set out," Morys said as he showed her how to do it using a flint. "If your lamp should go out, you'll have to find another lantern lighting station somewhere along the way. The electric lights haven't yet been installed past the stable."

Morys set off into the dark tunnel with Bethan and Dobbin right behind him. Morys' and Bethan's headlamps cast a pale-yellow beam ahead that bounced off the roof and walls in rhythm with their footsteps. Even with the light from their helmets, the darkness in the tunnel seemed to want to swallow her. She slowed down and let Dobbin catch up until she was beside his head. She placed her right hand on his neck. The presence of her horse brought her comfort and a fair amount of courage. "I'll need your help, dear Dobbin," she whispered. Dobbin's ears twitched and he bobbed his head.

A short way down the tunnel, they stopped at a junction. The tracks split to both the right and the left as they headed down opposing tunnels. "We're going to the left. Come forward on the track and start walking down the track to the left. What is your command to your pit pony to tell him to turn left?"

"Come here," Bethan said.

"That's right," Morys said.

Bethan heard the wheels creak as Dobbin pulled the tram forward. When he reached the junction, he stepped over the tracks going to the right and stepped in the middle of the tracks turning to the left.

"Good boy, Dobbin," Bethan said as she rubbed his white stripe. "Tomorrow, I will bring you some apples."

Farther into the darkness they walked; how far Bethan could not guess. Eventually they came to a set of metal doors.

"These are called ventilation doors or 'air-doors'," Morys said, tapping one of the doors with his knuckle. "There are three sets of them between here and the coal face."

"What are they for?" Bethan inquired, her large eyes scanning the doors and the metal frame that held them in place.

"They're an important part of our ventilation system. They allow us to control the passage of fresh air around the mine. They're also a safety measure to keep dangerous gasses from polluting the entire mine."

Bethan's eyes widened.

Morys patted her shoulder. "Don't worry. Accidents rarely happen."

Having lived her entire life in a coal mining town, Bethan doubted this was true. But she forced herself to smile.

"The air-doors only open in one direction," Morys said. "Coming from the stables with your empty tram, you will need to open the doors toward you and let Dobbin walk through. On the way back, Thomas has taught Dobbin to nudge open the doors with his head all by himself."

The deeper into the mine they walked, the hotter and more humid it became. In some places Bethan walked through water up to her ankles. She wiped her forehead with her sleeve, and wished she had some water to drink.

Morys led Bethan and Dobbin all the way to the coal face where a full tram was waiting for them.

"This is the tumble-up. It is the hardest part of your job," Morys said. "You must first take the limber off, which connects Dobbin's harness to the tram. The men at the face will pull the empty tram off the track and push it to the space on the side called a 'pass-by'. You must instruct Dobbin to pivot his haunches around and back up to the full tram. Then you connect his harness to the new tram with the limber."

It took several minutes for this task to be completed. When the miners at the face had pushed and pulled the empty tram to the side, and the full tram was attached to Dobbin's harness, Morys and Bethan made the long hike back through the tunnels to the pit shaft. It took more than an hour for Dobbin to pull the heavy load to where it could be unhitched and hauled up the mine shaft. By this time, his coat was covered in sweat and coal dust. The white socks on two of his legs were black.

No time had been allowed for a bait-stand, and Bethan felt herself weak from hunger. She regretted leaving her choppy-box in the sorting area when she first came to work so many hours before. *I will not do that again,* she told herself. Then she looked over at Dobbin.

"Oh, Dobbin, you must be as tired and thirsty as I am." She threw her arms around his neck.

The final task was to clean and feed Dobbin back at the stable. The water she used to wash him was icy cold, but Dobbin didn't seem to care. He stood quietly, his eyelids drooping, and let the sweat and coal dust flow down his legs.

Bethan rubbed him dry with an empty burlap feed bag. She filled his manger with hay and gave him a large scoop of oats.

One by one, the other stalls were filled with returning ponies. The miners greeted her enthusiastically.

"How did Dobbin treat you?"

"I hear ye be Thomas' daughter. Best keep the fact that yer a girl a secret when the mine inspector comes 'round."

One of the more skeptical miners asked, "Do you think you can keep up?"

"Ye might want to tie a string around yer trousers," said another, "so the rats won't crawl up yer legs."

Chapter 12

Penallta Colliery at the end of the day

By the time Bethan entered the cage with several men to be carried to the top, she was struggling to keep her eyes open. Her stomach ached from hunger. Her skin felt wet and gritty.

As the cage jostled its way up to the top of the shaft, she leaned against the side and closed her eyes. She sighed as she wondered how she was going to be able to do this. She reminded herself that other children her age had successfully toiled in the mines. She needed to persevere to help her father, no matter how hard it was. A silver lining appeared as she told herself that at least she would have Dobbin at her side.

When the cage jerked to a stop at the pit head, the men hustled out, leaving Bethan alone. She held her breath and walked out the gate.

"Bethan," a voice called out to her.

She lifted her eyes and looked toward the direction from which the sound came. Dylan stood a short distance away, a welcoming smile on his face, his arm extended holding her choppy-box. "I'll wager you're famished," he said.

◆ ◆ ◆ ◆ ◆ ◆ ◆ ◆ ◆ ◆

Catrin was waiting in the yard at home, looking down the street and watching Bethan and Dylan slowly approaching. Her hands twisted the white apron she was wearing even as relief at their appearance flowed through her.

"Bethan, what kept you so long?" she said as Bethan reached the front of their garden. She hurried forward and put her arms around her daughter. "I've been so worried about you."

Catrin pulled off Bethan's cap, letting her long brown hair fall over her shoulders. "You look so tired, my child." Turning to Dylan, she added, "Thank you, lad, for bringing her home again."

"I shall do so every day, ma'am."

"You best be running along now. I'm sure your mam will be worried about you as well."

"Yes ma'am," Dylan said. "I will be waiting for you in the morning, Bethan."

"Thank you," Bethan said. "For everything."

"And I'm a bit jealous, you know," he said over his shoulder as he walked away.

"What did he mean by that?" Catrin said as she helped Bethan out of her dust covered clothing by the back door to the house.

"By what, Mam?" Bethan said. Barely able to stand, she clutched the door frame.

"That he's jealous?"

"I'm a haulier now."

Catrin jolted upright. "What? A haulier? But that means . . ."

"I'm working underground. Yes." Bethan closed her eyes and leaned her head against the door.

"How can that be? It's against the law for girls and women to work underground."

"They need me. Dobbin needs me."

"Dobbin?"

"Father's horse."

"Yes, I know. But what does he have to do with it?" she said, her voice getting sharp.

"No one else can handle him."

"And they expect a little girl to do it? What are those men thinking? They shall hear from me, they will!"

"No, Mam. Please. If Dobbin won't work, I fear what might happen to him."

Catrin felt her anger subsiding as she looked at her exhausted little girl. She looked so young and tiny

. . . and dirty. Yet a strength exuded from her child that she had never seen before. She had to remind herself that her dreams for her talented daughter to get an education, maybe even a university degree, were just on hold—only until her husband was healed. She wrapped her arms around Bethan and stroked her hair. "You love that horse."

Bethan nodded.

"And he will work for you?"

Bethan nodded again as she fell asleep in her mother's arms.

Chapter 13

Penallta Colliery, the third day in the mine

The next day, Bethan stepped into the cage, already full of miners. They pressed together to give her room and welcomed her with warm greetings.

"Thomas' daughter," she heard one of them whisper to another.

The cage landed on the floor of the pit with a bump, and the men streamed out. Bethan walked silently along with them, listening to their heavy footsteps on the stone ground. On occasion, one of the miners addressed her.

"Glad to see you got some yorks on your trouser legs, young lady. I'd hate to have the rats eat you for lunch," said one tall, muscular man.

"Ah, don't scare the lass," said another as several chuckles rippled through the crowd.

"She's Thomas' daughter. She won't scare that easily," said the first. "Am I right, miss?"

Bethan looked up, all the way to his eyes, and forced a smile.

"See. I told you." He gave her a gentle pat on her head, then walked away whistling.

Bethan arrived at the stables with several other hauliers. "Dobbin," she said as she approached his stall.

Dobbin turned his head, his soft brown eyes welcoming her.

Bethan pulled a chunk of apple from her pocket, placed it on her outstretched hand, and waited for him to take it.

His soft lips wiggled as they took it from her hand.

Morys approached the stall carrying Dobbin's harness. "Let's see if you can do it alone today," he said with a smile.

Piece by piece, beginning with a leather collar that went over his head and rested at the base of his neck, she placed the parts of the harness where they belonged. The shafts were connected to one another at the rear with a metal bar and were quite heavy for a young girl. She had to drag them in place and get Morys' help lifting them to the right height. She finished by attaching the bands that ran over his back to the U-shaped shafts between which Dobbin stood. Just when she thought she was done, Morys reminded her of the head gear used to protect his head and eyes.

Once everything was in place, Morys walked around, inspecting her work. Bethan stood at Dobbin's head and waited.

"Fine work, young lass," he finally said.

Bethan breathed out a sigh and gave Dobbin a rub on his neck.

"Let's grab a limber pin and hook him to the draw bar on the tram," Morys said.

Bethan was the last of the hauliers to leave the stable. She went into the choppy room to get a feed bag for Dobbin. As she grabbed a metal scoop and reached into the bin of chaff, she heard a rustling sound. Suddenly, a large grey rat scurried up her arm, his claws gripping the sleeve of her shirt, and leaped to the ground, disappearing behind a pile of hay. Bethan screamed and dropped her scoop. She slid down, buried her face in her hands, and cried.

Dobbin, standing patiently in the aisleway, let out a deep, throaty, nicker.

Wiping away her tears, Bethan looked up. "It's okay, Dobbin," she said, sniffling. "I'm coming."

Bethan's thoughts went to her father. *He needs me. He put up with the rats. I can, too.* She stood and finished scooping Dobbin's lunch into the feed bag and left the room.

She lit the flame on the small oil lamp and attached it to her cap. Stepping into the center of the track, she took a deep breath and let it out slowly before she said, "Go on."

Chapter 14

Hengoed, May 1938

Two weeks went by, and the spring flowers were in full bloom. The sun rose higher in the sky, bringing a cheerful yellow glow to the light surrounding the village of Hengoed.

Bethan and her mother walked home from church services, hand in hand. Bethan closed her eyes and let the sun rest on her cheeks. She breathed in deeply of the fresh air. It felt good to be clean and out in the daylight, something she didn't see all week.

"We shall visit your father after lunch," her mother said.

"Bethan," a voice behind her called out.

Bethan stopped at the sound of Dylan's voice. Turning, she watched him run up to her. "I didn't know you had such long hair," he said.

Bethan blushed and pushed her light brown locks back over her shoulders.

"I didn't know you had freckles," she joked. "Can't see them under the coal dust."

"Join us for lunch, won't you, Dylan?" Catrin said.

"Thank you, ma'am," he responded with a smile that reached his eyes.

* * * * * * * * * *

Bethan and her mother walked down the hallway in the hospital. Bethan wrinkled her nose at the sharp odor of disinfectant. Their sturdy shoes clicked on the gleaming tiles covering the floor. The bright florescent bulbs, newly popular in Wales, hummed overhead. This was a far different environment from the one in which she spent her days. *No rats*, she thought. *What a relief.*

Finding her father's room, she pushed open the door.

Thomas lay on his bed reading a book. At the creak of the door, he looked up. His initial smile was immediately replaced by a frown. "You look so pale, Bethan," he said, his eyes filled with worry.

"But Tad, there isn't much sunshine underground, you know," she said, forcing a smile.

Thomas shook his head and looked down at his legs. "It shouldn't be much longer. They reset the bones this week and put on new casts. Just a couple more months, I suspect." He looked over at his beautiful little girl. "Can you manage that long?"

"Yes, Tad. I have Dylan to walk with me to and from the mine, and Dobbin to take care of me during the days."

"I'm so glad of that," he said, reaching for her hand. "How is my old friend, Dobbin?"

"He's wonderful. He works so hard."

Catrin bent over her husband and gave him a kiss on the forehead. "You look better today," she said.

"Aw, don't lie, it doesn't become you," Thomas said before pulling her down for a kiss on her lips.

Turning his attention back to Bethan, he cautioned, "Always listen to your pony. They seem to have a sixth sense as to the presence of danger. It was Dobbin who saved my life. If he hadn't warned me that the roof was about to cave in, I wouldn't be here today."

Chapter 15

ethan and her mother both overslept the next day. If Dylan hadn't banged on the door, they might never have awakened, so tired were the two of them.

"Bethan! Bethan," her mother called up the stairway. "Hurry. You'll be late."

Bethan jolted awake and jumped out of her bed. Throwing on her trousers, shirt, and vest, she dashed down the stairs.

Dylan was standing in the doorway as her mother was cutting bread and cheese to place in her choppy-box.

"Fill your tin with water," Catrin said as she scurried around the kitchen. "I put in some extra bread since you haven't had any breakfast."

With a hug and kiss on her forehead, Bethan was scooted out the door by her mother.

When one routine is disrupted, it has a way of affecting the whole day. Bethan hurried to the stable, noticing that all the other hauliers were already gone with their pit ponies and trams. "Dobbin," she called out. It was answered by a throaty nicker.

She rushed through putting on the harness and hooking Dobbin to the empty tram. She lit her oil lamp and stepped over the rail to the center of the track. "Go on, Dobbin," she said. "Go on." Lifting her booted feet, she walked forward. Dobbin dutifully followed behind.

By the time they reached the seam, Bethan's stomach was complaining about the lack of breakfast. She performed all the necessary duties to switch the empty tram for the full one, then started back to deliver it to the pit.

Weakened from hunger, she trekked doggedly toward the first set of air-doors. She slowed her steps and moved to Dobbin's shoulder as he used his muzzle to push the doors open. The doors shut with a bang behind them.

Bethan stopped. "It's grub-time, Dobbin." Reaching for her choppy-box, she realized she had not filled a feed-bag for Dobbin. "Oh, Dobbin, I'm so sorry. I forgot your lunch." Dobbin cocked his head to one side, as if in disbelief. "It's okay," she added, giving him a kiss on the nose. "I'll share mine."

She crouched down with her back against the wall of the tunnel. Breaking her bread into small pieces, she held one out to Dobbin. He lowered his big head and gently took it from her hand.

As they ate, Bethan heard the scuffling sounds of rats nearby. She jerked her head from side to side, casting the beam from her lamp first one way and then another, in search of the unwelcome visitors.

To one side, Bethan's light shone on the largest, blackest rat she had ever seen in the mine. His eyes glowed menacingly. His whiskers moved up and down as his nose twitched. Crouched low, he crept toward her. Not a meter away, he stopped and sat on his back haunches, his front paws lifted to reveal sharp claws.

"Go!" Bethan cried, her voice quivering and her hands trembling. "Leave me be, you nasty beast."

Suddenly, her lamp went out. Bethan and Dobbin were left in complete darkness. She heard a squeak and felt a furry creature leap onto her lap. In the same instant, the invader snatched the bread right out of her fingers.

Screaming, she leaped up and flailed her arms through the thick blackness, trying to find Dobbin. Her right hand connected with his head, and she draped her arms around his neck. Still quivering, heart pounding, she let herself crumple against him and bury her face in his mane. "Dobbin. Oh, Dobbin," she moaned. "What are we going to do now?"

Dobbin tossed his head, making the buckles on his harness jingle, and took a step forward. Bethan straightened and stepped back, stumbling over the rail and nearly falling.

Bethan heard Dobbin take another step.

"Can you get us back?" Bethan said. "Even in this darkness?"

Dobbin took another step.

She reached forward, running her hands along the shaft. She climbed up on his back, leaned over the collar, and pressed her upper body against the crest of his neck. "Go on," she said, her voice shaking.

Step by step, Dobbin, with Bethan on his back, pulled the heavy tram through total darkness. The screeching sound of rusty wheels on the tracks and the rhythmic movement of Dobbin's shoulders were the only indication they were moving forward. Bethan's heart slowly stopped pounding, and her breathing became more even as she allowed herself to put her trust completely in Dobbin.

Riding the pit ponies was strictly against the rules of the mine. She had been warned by Morys that riding the horse or the shaft iron that connected Dobbin's harness to the tram would get her fired. But in this dark, wet, musty cavern, she didn't much care.

It was a long journey to the next air-doors. Invisible to Bethan, Dobbin must have sensed their presence, for he pushed them open without difficulty. Beyond the doors, a small glimmer of light appeared ahead. Bethan recognized it as the lamp-lighting station Morys had pointed out their first trip to the seam. It was there that miners could refill their oil lamps and light the wick.

In this section of the tunnel, the roof was higher, and Bethan could sit up on Dobbin's back without fear of hitting her head. She kept her eyes glued to the tiny glow ahead.

Dobbin must have recognized it as well, for his steps quickened and he stopped as soon as they arrived at the source of the light.

Bethan swung her right leg over Dobbin's back and stood on the shaft. She pulled her lamp out of the loop of fabric that held it to her helmet, filled it with oil and held the wick to the flame of the lantern. Immediately, her lamp began to glow. Setting it back in its secure position on her cap, she jumped down to the uneven tunnel floor.

"That's much better, isn't it, Dobbin?" she said, rubbing her horse's face and giving him a kiss on his soft muzzle. "Thank you for getting us here." A tear escaped her eye, and she brushed it away, leaving a black streak on her cheek.

"Let's have a little more to eat," she said. She looked around and only then realized she had left her choppy-box behind. "Oh, no!" she moaned. "Now the rats will eat it!"

Little did she know they already had.

Chapter 16

Bethan and Dylan walked home, enjoying the setting sun as it warmed their faces. They both found themselves squinting and shielding their eyes as they struggled to adjust to the brightness.

Most of the time, the two friends spoke very little as they trudged home. But on this day, the sunshine filled Bethan with an energy that had long been buried.

"I miss the sun," Bethan said.

"Yes. I do, too," said Dylan.

Bethan looked over at her friend. "Do you want to keep working in the mine when you grow older?"

Dylan stopped. His eyes sparkled. "Oh no. I have dreams. I want to become a builder and work with wood instead of rock. I've been collecting tools, and many evenings I practice woodworking with my uncle who is a cabinet maker."

Bethan's hazel eyes opened wide. "Dylan, you never told me that before."

"I guess it just never came up." Dylan started walking, his head down. "Do you think that's silly?"

"Oh, no. I think that's wonderful." She reached over and took his hand. "I'm going to go to the university someday. I want to become a veterinarian and work with horses."

Dylan smiled. "How will a haulier do such a thing?"

"I'm going back to Hengoed County Girls' School in the fall . . . if my father is healed and we can afford the tuition."

Dylan squeezed her hand. "You know, Bethan, it wouldn't surprise me one bit if you did go to university."

Bethan lifted her chin and looked at the gold and pink sunset. "Oh, I will. I will."

Years later, as Bethan recalled that conversation with her friend, she realized that was the moment when her ambition to become a veterinarian was solidified.

◆ ◆ ◆ ◆ ◆ ◆ ◆ ◆ ◆ ◆

Dylan waved goodbye once Bethan reached the garden walk that led to her cottage. She pushed open the door and immediately heard a familiar cough.

"Tad!" she cried. Dropping her choppy-box, the same one that had been left in the tunnel and later recovered, she ran into the little parlor and skidded to a stop, surprised at what she saw. Propped up in a chair by the fireplace, Thomas was waiting for her, his arms opened wide in welcome. She flew into them.

"Oh, my little peach," he said, casting off her dusty cap and letting her locks fall down her back. "I will have my beautiful daughter back soon."

She buried her head in his shoulder as he stroked her hair. "Tad. You are home at last." Tears of joy welled in her eyes.

"Yes, my little peach. The doctors said I can finish healing at home." He coughed, then cleared his throat. "They tell me you are doing a remarkable job with Dobbin."

Bethan sat up. "Dobbin is wonderful, Tad. He has stolen my heart."

"Yes. A special horse, that one. Oh, how I wish he didn't have to spend all his days far underground."

Bethan nodded. "I often dream of him."

"Do you? And what do you dream?"

"I dream that he is running free across a meadow filled with flowers. The bluebirds flutter around him and I . . ." she stumbled to a halt, blushing.

"Go on, child. What do you do?"

"I sing his lullaby and he turns and comes to me."

"And then . . .?

"Oh, Tad. You know me too well."

"Let me guess. You climb on his back, clutch his mane, and ride him into the sunset."

Bethan and Thomas filled the tiny house with the sound of their giggles.

Chapter 17

Penallta Colliery a few days later

With the end of her toil in the mines finally in sight, Bethan felt the gradual release of the heavy burden she had been shouldering the previous months. Even the tunnels didn't seem so dark. Yet by the end of each day, the last load of coal from the seam seemed to be harder and the journey to the pit seemed longer. Her feet dragged as she walked in front of Dobbin, often tripping over loose rocks or the uneven ground.

A few days after Thomas returned home, Bethan was leading Dobbin toward the pit after picking up a full tram at the coal seam. They were making good progress until they went through the second set of air-doors. After the doors banged shut, Bethan looked ahead. She noticed a jumble of trams sitting askance across the rails. Four tubs had become entangled and derailed. Several miners were climbing around the pile-up, cursing and shouting. Noticing Bethan, one of the miners said, "Forgive me my blasphemy, lass. 'Tis no excuse for that."

Bethan stood, wide-eyed as she watched the men try to untangle the mess. Afraid to ask what happened, she merely listened. Soon, the story unfolded.

One of the largest pit ponies, an impressive gelding named Boxer, stood at over fifteen hands. Because of his strength, he was often required to pull two fully-loaded trams from another seam. This day, he was tasked with taking two trams from the coal seam down a fairly steep incline. This demanded extra effort to keep control as the trams pushed against him. With each step, he had to brace himself, using every ounce of strength to prevent the heavy load from overpowering him. To alleviate some of the strain, his haulier used the sprag, inserted in the tram's wheels, as a break every few meters.

All was proceeding well until two trams from the face broke away before they were hitched to the waiting pit pony. They came hurtling down the hill from behind them. The haulier, in a desperate attempt to avoid the oncoming danger, leaped to one side and threw himself to the ground. The runaway trams thundered right over him without hitting him. But they collided mercilessly into Boxer's trams.

The impact was devastating. The force of the collision knocked Boxer off his feet. The wooden shams splintered and broke, piercing the gelding's side. In the ensuing chaos, the four trams continued down the hill, crushing Boxer, and derailing in the process.

Beneath the rubble, with a groan of pain, Boxer took his last breaths—a valiant pit pony tragically brought down by the perils of the mining world.

All four trams had to be unloaded piece by piece with the coal being placed in empty trams farther down the track. Then the empty trams were untangled and lifted off Boxer's body.

At the sight of the dead horse, Bethan gasped and buried her face in her hands. One of the miners knelt in front of her and took her hands in his. "I'm sorry ye had to see this, lass. 'Tis a horrible thing that happened to such a noble beast. He will be missed by all of us."

Bethan sniffled and nodded.

Other miners stepped up to her, attempting to offer words of comfort.

"Accidents do happen in the mines. They're a dangerous place for both man and beast. Yer father can attest to that," said one.

"His toil is finished, and he is freed from this God-forsaken tomb," said another one.

Boxer's haulier sat by his head and wept openly.

Bethan closed her eyes as the men cut Boxer into small enough pieces to fit into a tram. He was taken out of the mine for the last time, never to see the sunshine or nibble the fresh grass again.

◆ ◆ ◆ ◆ ◆ ◆ ◆ ◆ ◆

It took many days for Bethan to be able to sleep through the night. Her father, hearing her cries, rocked her to sleep and sang her lullaby.

Close your eyes, little one,
'neath the Welsh moon's gentle glow,
In the meadow where the ponies
softly wander to and fro.
Hush now, dear child,
let the night breeze gently sigh,
As the stars above tell tales of ponies trotting by.

Chapter 18

Several days after witnessing Boxer's death, Bethan was still struggling with the visions playing out in her head. Her only source of comfort was being with Dobbin. She sang her lullaby as she harnessed Dobbin. Her sweet voice filled the stable and echoed down the tunnel.

Suddenly, a large man with a thick mustache and bulging stomach appeared beside Dobbin's stall. "Excuse me, haulier, may I ask your name?" he said.

Startled, Bethan froze in the middle of latching Dobbin's head-gear. She stopped singing and turned slowly toward the man. He was not a man she had ever seen at the mine before.

"I asked you your name."

"Yes, sir. It's Bethan, sir."

He stepped forward as Dobbin snorted a warning. As he snatched her cap from her head, her hair tumbled down. "A girl," snorted the man in disgust. "A girl in the mine." He shoved the cap toward her.

Taking the cap from his hand, Bethan clutched Dobbin's halter to steady herself. "Yes, sir. I am Thomas' daughter. I'm working his shift with Dobbin while he heals from the accident that sent him to the hospital."

"No excuses, lass. It's against the mining laws for a girl to work underground. You will cease what you are doing and follow me immediately."

Dobbin stomped a back hoof and the man hustled out of the stall, out of harm's way.

Bethan's heart began pounding. Her hands started shaking. "I'll be back," she whispered to Dobbin. "Wait for me."

With head bowed and cap in hand, Bethan followed the large man to the cage at the mouth of the pit. The ride up seemed to take an eternity as he stood beside her, his arms folded across his chest, his breathing fast and loud.

Exiting the cage, he stomped off in the direction of the mine manager's office, Bethan following. As they passed the sorting area, she caught Dylan's eye. He cocked his head and mouthed, "What's going on?"

She shook her head and pursed her lips.

Reaching the office, the man pounded his fist on the door. Not waiting for an acknowledgment, he twisted the doorknob and barged in. Bethan followed. The door swung closed behind them.

"What is the meaning of this?" the inspector said without preamble.

The manager jumped up from his chair. "Inspector? I wasn't expecting you today."

"Apparently not," he said, burying his fists in his sides.

"What is the meaning of what?" the manager said, his voice shaking.

The inspector stepped aside, exposing Bethan who was standing behind him, quivering.

The manager slumped back into his chair, burying his head in his hands.

"You realize that this will mean a hefty fine for the Penallta mine and will probably cost you your job!" his voice rising, a sneer spreading across his face.

The workers, including Dylan, had stopped their work, and gathered outside the door, listening to the heated conversation going on in the office.

"Excuse me, step aside. Let me pass," Morys said.

The workers parted ways and let the well-respected ostler move up to the door.

Morys opened the door and entered the office.

"Sir. May I speak?"

The inspector turned. "And who might you be?"

"I am Morys, the ostler here at the Penallta mine."

"So, you are as culpable as your manager," the inspector said. "What can you possibly have to say in your defense of allowing a little girl underground? Are you aware that is strictly forbidden by the Mining Act of 1842?"

"Yes, sir. I am."

"Well then? What can you say that will interest me?"

"Sir, Bethan is the daughter of our best haulier."

"So, I hear. But what does that have to do with it?"

"Thomas was severely injured when a section of the roof collapsed several months ago."

"That happens. All the more reason for the law."

"Yes, sir, I understand. But their family has been without a source of income since the accident."

"We are not heartless people, young man. We have made allowances for that. Women and girls may work at the mine but must remain above ground," he said, lifting his chin pompously.

"But Dobbin needs me," Bethan said in a barely audible whisper.

The inspector turned his attention to the girl. "What did you say, young lady?"

Morys stepped up to Bethan and placed a comforting arm over her shoulders. "She merely spoke the truth. She said Dobbin needs her."

"Dobbin? Is that the pit pony?"

"Yes, sir."

"Well, that is just a pile of horse manure if I ever heard one. All that horse needs is food, water, and a master to tell him what to do!" the inspector said, bringing his fist down on the desk with a bang.

"I can tell you don't work with horses, sir," said Morys.

"Not unless I must, young man," he said, his eyes as hard as coal.

"Well, sir, horses have their own personalities and their own peculiarities," said Morys. "As it happens, Dobbin is a rather intelligent horse that has strong preferences about who he will work for."

"Isn't that what a whip is for?" sneered the inspector.

"Dobbin doesn't respond well to a whip," Bethan said.

The inspector turned on Bethan. "I'll trust you to not interfere with our discussion, child."

Bethan dropped her chin and shuffled her feet, flushing.

"As the child said, Dobbin doesn't respond well to a whip," Morys said. "Bethan's father, Thomas, was Dobbin's haulier. When the horse was injured nearly a year ago, Bethan helped nurse him back to health. When Thomas was injured, Bethan came to the mine to work."

"I initially placed her in the sorting section," interjected the manager.

"But no one else could handle Dobbin," Morys said. "So, the manager and I decided to give Bethan a try in hopes that we wouldn't have to discard an expensive asset for the mine."

"Lovely story. But I still maintain that the law has been broken," said the inspector, clearly not moved. "I have no choice but to levy a substantial fine on the mine and insist that this girl be returned to the sorting section."

Chapter 19

Penallta Colliery the next day

The only person even slightly happy about having Bethan assigned back to the sorting line was Dylan.

"I've missed working beside you, Bethan," Dylan said as they walked slowly home. "But I'm sorry to see you so unhappy."

"I have missed you, too. But my only concern is what will become of Dobbin," she said, brushing away a tear.

"Won't they continue using him as a pit pony?"

"Not if he won't let any of the other hauliers lead him."

"But what of your father? He can handle him."

"Yes, but Tad won't be back to work for at least another month. How long will the mine owner feed and care for a horse that won't work?"

Dylan dropped his head and kicked a stone ahead of him. "I see what you mean. Not long, I would guess."

◆ ◆ ◆ ◆ ◆ ◆ ◆ ◆ ◆ ◆

The next day the manager found Bethan at her station where she was raking coal. "Bethan, can you come to my office, please?"

Bethan looked up in surprise. "H - have I done s-something wrong, sir?" she asked.

"Oh no. There is something I want to discuss with you."

Bethan set her rake down, feeling her heart pounding in her chest. She looked over at Dylan, whose raised eyebrows and cocked head showed he was as curious as she. "See you soon, Bethan," he whispered.

Bethan followed the mine manager to his office. He opened the door and motioned her inside. Standing in the middle of the room was Morys.

"Oh, Morys!" she exclaimed. "Is Dobbin alright?"

"For the time being, yes. But he misses you," he said, removing his cap and scratching his head.

"Is he willing to work?" Bethan said, her hands clutched and pleading.

"Not yet. No one has been able to win him over. Truth be told, few are willing to try."

Bethan dropped her head. "I'm so sorry to hear that. I wish I could help."

"As do I, Miss. As do I," Morys said.

The manager stepped in. "Tell her your idea."

Bethan lifted her head and looked into Morys's eyes. She held her breath and waited.

"Bethan, the horse show season is nearly upon us. Two weeks from now will be the local Flower Festival in the village. There's always a horse show at the festival. There has been a class for the exhibiting of pit ponies for nigh on a hundred years. Collieries from all over Wales and England show off their finest ponies at their local festivals. Those that perform well can be entered in the Royal Show and eventually at the International Horse Show in Olympia."

The manager jumped in. "We would like Dobbin to represent the Penallta Colliery at the shows."

Bethan's eyes opened wide, and her jaw dropped. "Dobbin?" She looked back and forth between the two men.

Morys grinned and bobbed his head enthusiastically. "And the best part is—we want you to handle him at the shows!"

"Oh. Oh, my! I can't believe it," Bethan said, moving carefully over to a chair and sitting down. Clutching the arms of the chair, she looked up. "Is this truly happening?"

Morys laughed. "Yes, it's truly happening. But we have work to do to get him ready for the shows."

Chapter 20

The very next day, Bethan was lowered down the pit in the cage once again. She put on a helmet and ran to the stables. A smile filled her face as she smelled the familiar musky odor of horses and leather. Turning into the stable she slowed to a walk and started singing her lullaby. From down the aisleway she heard a familiar nicker.

"Dobbin! Dobbin, it's me. I told you to wait for me and here I am." She stepped into his stall and up to his head. Brushing his forelock out of his eyes she rested her forehead against his jaw and let the tears wet her cheeks. "I've come to take you home, Dobbin."

Bethan put on his head collar and clipped a lead to the brass ring under his chin. "Come back," she said.

Dobbin obediently shuffled his feet backwards, out of the stall.

Bethan led him out of the bright lights of the stable and into the dark tunnel that led to the pit, feeling her excitement mounting with each step. She felt like she was releasing a prisoner from his shackles—and in a way, she was. She slid her hand in her pocket to make sure the bit of carrot was still there. It was, and she smiled.

When they reached the pit, the cage was waiting for them. The miners had attached wooden sides to the cage. "We've found the horses are less likely to hurt themselves if we put up wooden walls," said one miner.

"Thank you," said Bethan. "Do you usually have a difficult time taking the pit ponies up?"

"Well, let's just say it isn't their favorite thing to do," said another as he opened the gate. "Just try leading him on in. Once he's in, we'll shut the gate, then you'll need to climb out."

"I can't ride up with him?"

"Oh, no. That would be much too dangerous. If he should start kicking you could get hurt."

Bethan looked over at Dobbin with his trusting brown eyes. She rubbed his forehead. "Go on," she said, giving him a slight tug on the lead.

Dobbin stepped up to the open gate and stopped. He pricked his ears forward and snorted loudly.

"It's okay, Dobbin. Go on," Bethan said as she lifted her foot and stepped into the box. "Go on."

Dobbin lifted one hoof and placed it on the platform with a loud thud that shook the cage. He threw up his head and backed away.

Bethan held tightly to the rope, her feet sliding over the plank as Dobbin pulled. "Go on, Dobbin. I'm here. Go on."

Dobbin shook his head, his forelock falling over his eyes. He stopped and snorted again.

"Do you need us to give him a little encouragement?" one of the miners said, holding a riding crop in one hand and tapping it against the palm of his other hand.

"No. He'll come. I have my own way of encouraging him." Bethan pulled the carrot out of her pocket and extended her hand. Dobbin looked at it and his ears twitched again.

"It'll be okay, Dobbin. Go on. I have a treat for you."

Dobbin stretched his neck as far as it could go, attempting to reach the carrot. His feet didn't move.

Bethan giggled. "You can't get it until you step on the platform."

Dobbin took one step forward. "Good boy," Bethan said.

Dobbin took another step forward. "You're almost there," Bethan said.

Two more steps and Dobbin had both front feet on the platform. Bethan backed up until she was against the far wall. "Come get your carrot, Dobbin. Go on."

Dobbin stepped all the way into the cage and the men slammed the door behind him. He started, and for a moment, his attention was no longer on the carrot. He snorted and kicked one hind hoof at the back gate.

"Easy, boy. Here's your carrot," Bethan said, holding her flattened hand under his muzzle. He took it with his lips and began chewing, saliva dripping from the sides of his mouth.

"Climb out, miss. Let's get him up top," said one of the miners.

Bethan climbed out of the cage and the miners called up, "Bring him up."

At the top of the pit, two large horses began walking in a circle, turning the windlass that rolled up the chains attached to the cage. Slowly, the cage lifted from the ground and began its two thousand-foot ascent.

Bethan watched from beside it, holding her breath. Dobbin held still as the cage moved up. His legs were spread to the sides in order to keep his balance.

Soon he was too high for Bethan to see, but she kept her eyes on the cage anyway. The sound of the grinding metal from the turning windlass, and the clanking of the chains, was all she could hear.

Once Dobbin reached the top, the miners, who had been waiting for him, opened the gate and said, "Come back."

Dobbin moved back, testing the surface with each step. When his entire body was out of the cage, one of the miners grabbed his rope and moved him away from the edge of the pit. Another miner put the horses on the windlass back to work lowering the cage to bring Bethan up.

Dylan ran over to Dobbin and was waiting beside him when Bethan arrived at the top of the pit.

"Bethan, he's a beauty," Dylan said, his face beaming. "No wonder you are so fond of him."

Bethan grinned. "Isn't he something?" she said, going up to the miner and taking the lead from him. "Do you think he'll do well at the show?"

"He just needs a little spit and polish, but I'm sure he'll be a star," Dylan said. "Will he let me pet him?"

"Stretch out your hand and let him sniff you first."

Dylan did as he was told, chuckling as Dobbin rubbed his hand with his soft muzzle. "I've never been so close to a pit pony before," he said, grinning. He lifted his hand and stroked Dobbin's wide face.

Bethan and Dylan walked Dobbin home, one on either side of his head. Dylan's excitement matched Bethan's and they chattered all the way.

For Dobbin's part, he seemed happy to be in the fresh air and sunshine. He lifted his head, his eyes wide and sparkling, his ears pricked forward. Turning from side to side, he examined everything around him, from the trees alive with chirping birds, to the grasses and flowers swaying in the gentle breeze. He stopped and sniffed the air.

"Go on, Dobbin," Bethan said with a giggle in her voice.

Dobbin dropped his head and gave her a nudge as he stepped forward.

Chapter 21

The entire village of Hengoed was abuzz with activity as everyone became involved in preparations for the annual Flower Festival. Every window box was overflowing with newly planted annuals—geraniums and petunias, mostly. Large pots in front of every store and house were now filled to the brim with flowers of all colors, shapes and sizes.

Bakers were preparing their favorite desserts. Artists were putting their finishing touches on paintings. Sidewalks and windows were washed, removing a year's worth of coal dust. Fresh coats of colorful paint were applied to doors. Anticipation filled the air.

Just outside of town, Bethan's home was immersed in the excitement as well. Once Dobbin had settled into his paddock in her backyard, a place he surely remembered from his time of convalescing, the work of turning a pit pony into a show horse began.

Morys came to Bethan's house each afternoon. He wanted to prepare both Bethan and Dobbin for what they would experience at the horse show. He explained that horse shows are divided into competitive events called 'classes' in which horses and riders or handlers demonstrate their skills according to specific criteria. These criteria can vary depending on the discipline. Hunters are judged differently than jumpers. Pleasure horses are judged differently than carriage horses. And so forth. Dobbin was registered in the Pit Pony class. He wouldn't be competing against jumpers or carriage horses.

The first task was teaching Bethan the rules of etiquette at a horse show and what would be expected of her and Dobbin in the ring. She was warned that many collieries would be sending their best horses and handlers to the show. The rivalry between the mine owners and horse handlers was intense. The owners wanted to show off their horses. The handlers wanted to show off their skills. Therefore, horses and hauliers needed to look their finest as well as behave their best. Some judges had even been known to use a white glove to test the cleanliness of the horses. Morys told Bethan that the hauliers would be dressed in their Sunday finest. For Bethan, that meant her best dress, shoes, and even a hat.

Morys demonstrated the proper way of leading her pit pony past the judges. She was taught when to stop and wait, and how to get him to obey using only her voice commands. She practiced harnessing him and hitching him to a tram so she would be ready when the judges watched her put him through his paces in that part of the pit pony competition. Since there were no rails in the arena, different wheels were attached to the tram so Dobbin could pull it through the soft dirt.

After each practice session, Morys helped her trim his mane and braid it with colorful ribbons. He showed her how to wash and brush the feathering, the long hairs on his lower legs, until they flowed smoothly over his hooves. His tail had been cut short while working in the mine to keep it from getting tangled in the harness. But Morys showed her how to braid the shortened hairs around the tailbone and interlace the braid with flowers.

On Thursday, before the first day of the festival, Dylan came to help her give Dobbin a bath. Catrin peeked around the laundry she was hanging on the line and watched the two friends splash the horse with soapy water, giggling the whole time. Two of

Dobbin's lower legs were white, and these took an extra amount of time to get clean. When they were finished, they stood back, their clothing dripping with soap and water, and looked at the results of their work while Dobbin eyed them warily.

"He looks like a new horse," Dylan said.

Catrin bent over and picked up her laundry basket. "I must say, the two of you are as clean as he is," she said with a wink.

"He looks like a show horse now," Bethan said with a giggle, her face beaming with pride. "Wait!" Bethan dashed into the cottage while Dylan held Dobbin's lead.

Soon, Bethan appeared at the door, standing behind her father who was seated in a wheelchair.

"How does he look, Tad?" she asked, though already sure of the answer.

"He's a champion for sure," Thomas said. "I'm so incredibly proud of both of you."

Chapter 22

*F*riday dawned bright and clear. The July weather was warm, perfect for the Flower Festival. The mine was closed for a three-day holiday, and the villagers were all gathering in town for the festivities. The idea of a respite from the hard labor in the mine filled everyone with excitement.

Music and singing filled the air with familiar Welsh folk songs. The sweet smell of pastries flowed from homes and bakeries. Children dashed to and fro, playing games of chase.

Dobbin had spent a leisurely night resting on the green grass of his paddock. Bethan hadn't slept.

Dylan arrived at Bethan's house early. Morys appeared shortly thereafter.

"He looks ready to show the world what he is made of, that's for sure," said Morys, examining Bethan's and Dylan's efforts. "Look at that sparkle in his eye. What's he trying to tell us, Bethan?"

Bethan rubbed his glistening neck. "He's telling us that he's ready to become the next champion."

◆ ◆ ◆ ◆ ◆ ◆ ◆ ◆ ◆ ◆

The Pit Pony Class at the horse show was scheduled to begin at noon. Morys pulled the tram to the show grounds. Dylan carried the leather harness. These would be needed if Dobbin made it to the finals. Bethan led Dobbin. Fellow miners from the Penallta mine cheered as Dobbin and Bethan walked by. Everyone in Hengoed wanted to see their local entrant win.

Arriving at the showgrounds, Bethan was surprised to see nearly a dozen pit ponies from nearby mines lined up for the class. Each was being handled by a big, strong man. As Morys had warned, the men were dressed in suits as though heading to church services. Each horse's coat gleamed in the sunshine. They were all beautiful.

Suddenly, the internal butterflies started their onslaught, and she lost the confidence she had been filled with just moments before. A wave of nausea flowed through her.

"I don't know if I can do this," she said to Morys as her trembling hand struggled to unbutton the top button of her nicest dress. Her fingers became entangled in her white lace collar. Finally giving up, she adjusted her hat on her head and smoothed her dress.

Morys set down the tram and hurried over to her. "Is this the girl who has been working in the coal mine these last months to support her family? Is this the girl who has put up with the darkness and the rats? Is this the girl who is the only one who can handle this horse?" He paused and smiled down at her. "Don't tell me you can't do this, because I won't believe you."

Bethan took a deep breath. Looking down, she nodded. "Okay," she whispered. She turned to Dobbin. "We can do this, Dobbin. We can show everyone what a great horse you are. You saved my father's life, after all! How many other pit ponies have done something as wonderful as that?"

When the class was called to enter the ring, Dylan gave Bethan a hug and Dobbin a pat on the shoulder. Morys took Bethan's hand and gave it a tight squeeze. He winked and said, "Off with ye, lass!"

Bethan and Dobbin were the fifth competitors to enter the arena. The announcer called out their names one by one. When he got to Bethan and Dobbin, there was a raucous cheer from the audience. Bethan looked around. It seemed the entire village of Hengoed was there watching her and

Dobbin. She had to fight the urge to run back out of the arena. Only her pride in Dobbin kept her going.

The handlers were instructed to line up down the center of the arena. One by one, the judges examined the horses. When they approached Bethan, one of them said, "Well, well, well, what have we here?"

The show secretary, holding a clipboard and pencil, was standing at the judge's elbow. "This is Dobbin, representing the Penallta Colliery."

"And the haulier?" asked the man, looking Bethan in the eyes.

"This is Bethan. She will be showing Dobbin today."

The judge's face softened. "Well, young lady. That is a mighty big horse you have there. Do you think you can handle him?"

"I'm sure I can, sir," Bethan said. She pursed her lips and clenched her jaw as she looked the judge in the eye.

"Alright then. Let's see what you have to show me today."

Bethan stood as motionless as a marble statue while the judges walked around and around Dobbin, making whispered comments for the secretary to jot down. Dobbin stood still, his weight evenly distributed on all four legs, his arched neck held high, his ears pricked forward, his eyes alert. At times the judges stopped and just stared at Dobbin, their fingers tapping their chins, nodding and conversing with one another.

When the judges moved on to the next horse, Bethan let out a long breath. She stared straight ahead, avoiding looking at the crowd of spectators.

When the judges had completed their examination of all the horses, they picked up the megaphone.

"We are pleased to announce our three finalists in the Pit Pony Class. They will go on to the next round of judging under harness. Our three finalists are from the following collieries. First, from New Rockwood, our newly opened mine." A cheer went up from a group of spectators sitting together while a man led his horse up to the judges' stand.

"Second, from Windsor." There was another cheer from the opposite side of the arena, and a second horse was led away from the line and up to the judges.

"And third, being shown by our first-ever female handler, Penallta."

The entire arena erupted. Bethan didn't move. She was aware of the cheering but couldn't get her body to respond. The crowd continued to applaud as the judge called her forward. "Penallta Colliery, please bring your pit pony forward."

Bethan blinked and bit her lower lip. The man handling the horse behind her stepped forward. "That's you, lass," he said, giving her a gentle push.

Chapter 23

Hengoed Flower Festival, day two

The Pit Pony Under Harness Class, the next requirement for the pit pony championship, was scheduled for the next day. Dylan, Morys and Bethan bedded Dobbin down in a stall in the barn just to the west of the arena. The entire time from when Bethan left the arena to making Dobbin comfortable in the stall, Dylan couldn't stop talking.

"Did you see those judges? They couldn't take their eyes off Dobbin."

Bethan smiled and nodded.

"Did you notice how much more beautiful and statelier Dobbin was compared to all the others?"

Bethan smiled and nodded.

"Did you hear the crowd when they announced you were in the finals?"

Bethan smiled and nodded.

"I thought you were going to faint."

This time, Bethan didn't smile.

◆ ◆ ◆ ◆ ◆ ◆ ◆ ◆ ◆ ◆

The next morning was spent polishing the harness, cleaning the tram, and redoing Dobbin's braids on his mane and tail. By noon, everyone on the team was convinced they were ready for the final round of the Pit Pony competition.

The finals were scheduled to start at 1:00 in the afternoon. Bethan made sure her dress was clean and her hat was on straight. She filled her pockets with apple slices while Morys put on Dobbin's harness and hooked up the tram with the limber pin.

Bethan walked up to Dobbin's head and slipped him an apple slice. "Now don't slobber on your harness," she said, giving him a pat on the neck.

Catrin appeared at her side and gave her a hug. "That was from Tad," she said. Then she slipped Dobbin a carrot. "That was also from Tad."

When the announcement came for their class, Bethan clenched her jaw and gave each of her team a tiny smile. She knew they couldn't see her knees knocking beneath her petticoats, but she hoped they wouldn't notice her shaking hands. "Go on," she said to Dobbin as she started walking toward the arena.

The three horses, one from the Windsor Colliery, one from the New Rockford Colliery, and one from the Penallta Colliery, entered the arena in full harness and pulling a tram. They all stopped in front of the judges.

The judges proceeded to give their instructions. "You will notice that we have set up a bit of an obstacle course. You are to maneuver around the course using only your voice commands. You are not to touch your pit pony." One of the judges proceeded to walk the course while the three handlers watched. Bethan was filled with doubts about Dobbin's ability to adjust to the difference between pulling a tram on the tracks through the tunnels, and this situation where the tram would be pulled across the ground. *Will it scare him? Would he still listen to my commands?* she wondered.

When he returned, the judge said, "Any questions?" There being none, he said, "Penallta Colliery will go first."

Bethan gasped. Then she rubbed her hands on her skirt, looked Dobbin in the eye, and said, "Go on." Dobbin lowered his head and pushed against the collar. Once they started moving, Bethan's nervousness vanished as she focused only on the task at hand.

The first obstacle was two poles placed just barely far enough apart for the tram to make it through. Bethan stepped through first. Dobbin looked at both poles, then hurried through without touching either one.

Next, several barrels were placed in a line. With Bethan calling out "gun on" to turn left and "come here" to turn right, Dobbin wove through the line of barrels like a slalom skier on a mountainside. When they reached the end of the line, Bethan said, "Come here back," and Dobbin turned around. They worked their way through the barrels going the other direction.

The final obstacle was a solid wall made from wood. They stopped in front of the structure and Bethan whispered, "You are a star, Dobbin. I'm so proud of you." Then in a loud voice she commanded, "Come back."

Just as he had done for Thomas, Dobbin pushed against the back of the shaft and moved the tram straight back.

Chapter 24

The celebration lasted well into the night. Friends and neighbors came by with casseroles and desserts and a feast was held. Chairs were set up in the backyard so everyone could be near the champion. Dobbin, wearing his blue ribbon around his neck, was treated to apples and carrots and lots of strokes.

Dylan and his parents brought their new camera to take a picture of Bethan with Dobbin. The 1930s had seen rapid developments in the field of photography. The Kodak Box Camera was one of the new inventions that allowed amateur photographers to enjoy taking pictures. Dylan and his father were two of those. The camera drew as much attention from the villagers as Dobbin did since few people in the village had ever seen one. For Dylan and his father, it was quite a luxury but one they were thrilled to own.

* * * * * * * * *

The next day, Morys met with Thomas, Catrin, and Bethan. Morys sat down at the kitchen table, beaming. Thomas rolled over in his wheelchair, his legs propped up in front of him. Catrin and Bethan took chairs and joined them.

Morys looked at Bethan and said, "I'm sure you know how pleased the manager and owner are that Dobbin won the show."

Catrin reached her arm around her daughter and gave her a hug. "Tad and I are so proud of you," she said, her eyes moist with tears.

"I always knew Dobbin was something special," Thomas said, looking at Morys. "Glad you gave him a chance to show his stuff."

"Well, it doesn't end here," Morys said, taking a sip of the tea Catrin had served him. "The mine owner and manager want to enter him in several more local shows but with their eye on the International Horse Show at Olympia. Several of the pit ponies we competed against at the Flower Festival will be attending the shows as well."

Catrin gasped. Thomas smiled. Bethan didn't respond.

"What's the matter, Bethan?" Morys asked. "Don't you want to go to Olympia with your horse?"

Bethan blinked and ran the fingers of one hand through her auburn curls. "I don't know anything about it."

"The International Horse show in Olympia, London, is one of the largest shows in the world," Thomas said.

"It started in 1888 as an agricultural show," Morys added, "but in 1907 it became exclusively a horse show. There will be show jumpers, dressage riders, carriage drivers, and exhibitions of horses from all over the world as well as the pit pony classes."

"There are always many pit ponies from South Wales entered," Thomas said. "Why, I was told that in 1931 sixty pit ponies came from the collieries around here."

"Oh, this is so exciting," Catrin gushed. "I've never been to London before." Then her hand flew to her mouth. "Oh. I'm sorry to be so presumptuous. Perhaps I'm not invited."

"Of course, you and Thomas would be invited as guests of the owner," said Morys. "Considering Bethan's age, it would only be proper for her parents to come." Turning his attention back to Bethan, he said, "Well, Bethan, what do you say? Shall we take Dobbin to Olympia with you as his handler?"

"I . . . I don't know what to say."

"Just say 'yes'," her father said.

"But what of Dobbin?" Bethan said.

"What do you mean?" Morys asked.

"Does that mean he will stay with me through the show season? Does that mean he won't have to go back to the mine?"

"We can't very well keep him in the pit between shows," Morys assured her. "He'd be up to his neck in filth and coal dust again. No, he'll have to stay here with you and Thomas. The owner is trusting you to take good care of him."

"Then my answer is yes!"

Chapter 25

Over the next few months, life changed for both Bethan and Dobbin. Summer went by in a whirl of grooming sessions and show performances at area festivals. Early most Saturday mornings, Bethan and Morys, and Dylan when he could get the day off, loaded Dobbin in a horsebox and drove to the site of the horse show. Each show was pretty much the same: the judges carefully examined Dobbin, then put Bethan and her horse through their paces.

In show after show, Dobbin came out on top.

Thomas went back to work at the colliery in September, enabling Bethan to stop working at the sorting tables and return to Hengoed County Girls' School. Dobbin was enjoying lolling around his paddock and making friends with the local birds and squirrels. The fresh air seemed to agree with him.

Each evening, Bethan returned from school, and Dylan returned from the colliery. They spent a couple of hours working together to keep Dobbin in shape for the weekend shows.

"Where are you taking Dobbin this weekend?" Dylan asked as he bent over to clean out a hoof.

"We're going to the festival in Newbridge."

"Oh. That's close."

"Yes. It's only about a half-hour drive," Bethan said as she brushed out Dobbin's tail. "That should make Dobbin happy. I don't think he likes the horsebox much."

"Can't say as I blame him. I don't think I'd like it either. I get sick just riding in a car. 'Course, I don't do it much." Dylan set Dobbin's hoof down and straightened up. "Do you think horses get motion sickness?"

"I don't know, but I do know they can't vomit if they have an upset stomach."

"They can't?"

"No. That's why it's so dangerous. Morys told me that a blockage in the stomach or intestines is called 'colic.' Many horses both above ground and in the mines can die from it."

"You sound like a veterinarian."

Bethan stopped brushing and looked at Dylan. "I have decided to become one."

"A coal miner's daughter with big dreams. I've always liked that about you."

Bethan put her hands on her hips and cocked her head to one side. "Don't you think I'll make it?"

"I have no doubt that you will," Dylan said.

Dylan approached Dobbin's head, clasped both sides of his headstall and looked him in the eye. "Don't you get that colic. You hear me, Dobbin?"

"After Newbridge comes Olympia," Bethan said, with a determination in her eyes that made Dylan smile.

◆ ◆ ◆ ◆ ◆ ◆ ◆ ◆ ◆ ◆

The International Horse Show at Olympia was the culmination of the show season in 1938. Riders in many disciplines came from all over the world to compete. It was where stars were made—both four-legged and two-legged.

The morning of the scheduled departure for London dawned cold and grey. The rain that had been falling during the night left Dobbin's paddock covered in mud. Bethan awakened early to feed Dobbin his breakfast, only to find him standing in a deep murky puddle. Bethan's and Dylan's work to clean up the horse the night before was all for naught.

"Oh, Dobbin, just look at you," she said when she saw him. "What will Morys say when he gets here?"

It was just a few minutes later that Morys drove around the cottage to the backyard. The truck Morys was driving was old and battered. The red paint faded to a pale pink. But the engine was strong enough to pull a horse and trailer, and that was all that mattered.

The wipers on the truck were working overtime to keep up with the rain. Leaving the engine running, he jumped out of the cab and sloshed across the yard.

"Oh, Morys, just look at Dobbin. He's a muddy mess," Bethan said.

Morys placed his hands on his hips and nodded. "That he is, lass. That he is." He shrugged and added, "There's nothing we can do about it now. We'll just have to clean him up when we get him in the barn at Olympia. Let's get everything loaded."

When everything they would need for the next few days was packed into the trailer and pickup, Bethan, Thomas and Catrin all squeezed onto the one bench seat beside Morys for the long ride to London.

Looking at the old Austin sitting beside the cottage, its tires flat, its body rusted, its windows black from coal dust, Morys said, "Sure wish you had that thing running, Thomas. It would be a more comfortable ride to London if we could take two cars."

Thomas nodded. "My father left me that car before The Great Depression. I've never had the money or the time to get it running."

Few colliery families had the luxury of owning a car. Most of the villagers in Hengoed had never even ridden in one. That's just the way things were in Hengoed.

Morys drove the pickup and trailer southeast out of Hengoed on the same two-lane road they had driven to get to Newbridge. But this time, they continued east on Route 30 all the way to London, crossing the River Severn before stopping to take a short break in Swindon. The break couldn't come soon enough.

"I can barely breathe," Catrin complained from where she was squeezed between Morys and Thomas.

"Aw," said Thomas, "but yer warm and dry. Be glad we didn't have to walk to London."

"Or ride Dobbin," added Morys, his eyes twinkling.

"I wouldn't mind riding Dobbin to London," Bethan said from where she was pressed against the door.

Thomas snorted. "Na, I'm sure you wouldn't."

The rain stopped after they crossed the River Severn and the fog lifted, making the drive easier for Morys and the views better for Bethan and her parents. They stopped at a small inn near the highway as they entered the outskirts of Swindon. None of them had ever seen this part of the country, having rarely left the confines of the Rhymney Valley, let alone crossed into England. Bethan couldn't contain her excitement as she looked out the windows and pointed out the sights. "Look at the beautiful river . . . I see a castle on that hill . . . Those farms are lovely . . . Look how big this city is!"

Morys found himself captivated by her infectious enthusiasm. "You believe this city is vast? Well, London will utterly dwarf it," he remarked with a smile. The ostler, a seasoned storyteller, eagerly delved into his experiences from his days serving in the British Army. He painted vivid pictures of the bustling streets of London, regaling them with tales of Buckingham Palace, the majestic residence of King George VI, freshly crowned just two years prior. "If you think Dobbin is beautiful, you should see the horses the palace guard ride. Those magnificent animals will take your breath away."

Chapter 26

After traversing two hundred forty-five kilometers (approximately 150 miles), they reached the expansive show facility hosting the prestigious Olympia International Horse show, nestled in the heart of West Kensington.

As they pulled into the show grounds, Bethan stared out the window, her mouth agape. She had never seen so many people or so many cars, trucks and horseboxes, and, most importantly, so many horses.

Morys pulled up in front of a large building. "I'll run in here and get our stabling assignment and show schedule."

While he was gone, Bethan got out of the truck. She breathed deeply of the crisp, winter air. She never knew air could smell so good. She looked at the enormous red brick building decorated with cream-colored pillars that housed the show offices, the stables, and the arena. A gigantic glass dome curved over the top of one part of the building, reminding her of the pictures she had seen of big city railroad terminals. She later learned that there was indeed a railroad station at the event center, but not under that big glass dome. The clip-clop of hooves created background percussion to the whinnies of horses and the excited voices of humans. She spun around, her arms spread wide.

"I love it here," she said.

Catrin and Thomas watched their daughter from the cab and smiled.

Morys returned, carrying a stack of papers. Climbing into the driver's seat, he said to Bethan, "Would you like to walk? You can follow us. I'll lead you to our barn."

"Oh, yes, please," Bethan said, happy to be out of the cramped truck and moving around. The energy was palpable and filled her soul with excitement. She skipped along behind the horsebox as Morys drove around to the back of the building. He stopped by an open door. "This is where we unload."

Bethan opened the back ramp of the horsebox and said, "Come back." Dobbin shuffled his feet, feeling for the ramp and knocking manure out as he went. When he reached the bottom of the ramp he stopped, lifted his head and let out a deep, throaty whinny. This was promptly answered by several other horses somewhere within the barn.

"What did they say?" Bethan said, patting Dobbin on the neck.

Dobbin answered with a quiet nicker.

"Oh, is that right? They welcomed you, did they?"

"Walk him around," Morys said. "He needs to stretch his legs. Your father and I will get his stall ready."

Thomas and Morys went into the barn with buckets, feed, and a bale of hay. Catrin followed them, her silence suggesting how stunned she was by the grandeur of it all.

Several other horses and ponies were also being led around. Bethan noticed two Welsh ponies, their winter coats clipped short, their long tails glimmering, their hooves polished. One was bright white. The other was chestnut and glowed like a new copper shilling. The girls, each about Bethan's age, approached Bethan and stopped.

One girl squinted her eyes and sneered. "What kind of a horse is that?"

"Shire, mostly," Bethan said.

"He's not a purebred?" asked the same girl. "He's so dirty. Oh, I bet he's one of the pit ponies. Well, don't let him shake that dirt off on my pony." With nose in the air, she marched off toward the barn, her spotless white pony trailing behind.

But the girl with the chestnut stayed where she was. "Don't pay her any mind," she said. "I think your horse is beautiful. He's so big and strong."

"Yes, he is," Bethan said. "He's had to work hard his whole life." She picked at some dried mud in Dobbin's mane. "I'm sorry he's so dirty. I had him all clean yesterday, but then the rainstorm came in."

"Would you like me to help you bathe him?" the girl asked.

Bethan's face brightened. "Oh, yes. I would love your help. He's a lot of horse to get clean. Are you sure?"

"I think it would be fun. Let me put Hardy away in his stall, then I'll come back and show you where the wash station is." The girl started to head for the barn, then turned back. "My name is Abigail. What's yours?"

"I'm Bethan, and this is Dobbin."

Chapter 27

The International Horse Show at Olympia

The show began the next day. Part of the day's events was a parade of the pit ponies in acknowledgment of the Olympia's original history as an agricultural show.

After hours of work the day before, Abigail and Bethan had Dobbin in tip-top shape. His mane was in short, tight braids, made perfect by Abigail's experienced hands, and decorated with colorful ribbons. His tail was also braided with ribbons and decorated with some flowers Catrin bought at a shop in the train terminal.

Morys came to Dobbin's stall when it was time to line up for the parade only to find the girls still fussing. Dobbin stood with a look on his face Morys couldn't read. Was he embarrassed? "So, what would your friends in the mine think of you now?" Morys chuckled, rubbing the white hairs that formed a stripe down Dobbin's face. "Is that what yer thinkin'?"

When they lined up to enter the arena with the other pit ponies, Bethan looked around. There had to be a hundred pit ponies of all different colors and sizes. She was surprised to see so many tiny ponies, some as small as twelve hands, and said so to Morys.

"The little Shetlands come from the north. Their coal seams are much narrower and the tunnels too small for horses like Dobbin."

"But how much coal can a little pony like that haul?"

"They're quite tough and strong for their size. But you're right. Our horses can get a lot more accomplished." He shrugged. "Our collier brothers in the north have to get by with what they have. They're far less productive than our mines in the south. That's why The Great Depression closed down so many collieries in the north. Most still haven't recovered."

Bethan looked at the ponies and smiled. "I'd like to take every one of them home with me."

Morys laughed. "I'm sure your father would appreciate that!"

The line of pit ponies began to move forward into the arena. When they entered, Bethan couldn't help but stop and gape. She had never seen anything so beautiful. The glass ceiling sparkled with sunlight. Flags and banners decorated the walls. Arena seating stretched to the rafters, and every chair was filled. Music blared over the loudspeakers. Spectators applauded politely.

Dobbin snorted, not accustomed to either the bright lights or the noise. Not sure he wanted to enter, he planted his front hooves.

"Hey, get movin'," said the haulier behind them.

Bethan glanced back. "Sorry, sir. We've just never seen anything like this before." She turned to Dobbin. "Go on."

Dobbin snorted again. "Please, Dobbin. Go on." Bethan felt her face getting hot.

Though still hesitant, Dobbin stepped into the arena and joined the parade.

The long line of pit ponies and their handlers wound around the perimeter of the arena, between the colorful jumps and the crowd of seated spectators. Bethan was leading Dobbin past a jump built to look like a brick wall when she heard someone shout, "Animal cruelty! Free the pit ponies." At the same moment, something flew through the air and hit Dobbin on the hindquarters . . . Hard.

Dobbin squealed and reared high in the air, pulling Bethan off her feet. The lead slipped through her hands as she fell to the soft surface of the arena. The moment Dobbin's front hooves returned to the ground, he started running, his lead trailing out behind. The parade came to a stop as handlers and horses watched the panicking horse. Several pit ponies danced around at the ends of their leads, putting an end to the orderly parade.

Bethan jumped to her feet, dust covering her best dress. "Dobbin!" she called. She watched as he darted around and between the jumps set up throughout the arena. The crowd let out a collective gasp then became silent. She took a deep breath to steady her nerves before calling out, "Gun on!"

Dobbin stopped, lifted his head, twitched his ears, then turned left between two post-and-rail jumps set close together.

"Go on," she shouted. Dobbin walked forward between the fences. Once he was past the jump standards, Bethan called out, "Come here." Dobbin turned right. One command at a time, Bethan guided him through the maze of jumps and back to her. When she reached out and grabbed the lead, the crowd stood and cheered.

Chapter 28

The International Horse Show at Olympia
- Day Two

The next morning, Bethan arrived at Dobbin's stall early to give him his morning feed and a fresh bucket of water, as well as to clean out his stall. As she was scooping manure and wet straw into the wheelbarrow, she heard Morys and two other men in a heated discussion.

"Did you see the article in today's *London Times?*" one man asked.

"I did indeed," Morys said. "It blamed Dobbin's outburst on poor training. No mention of the rock that was thrown, hitting him so hard it left a gash."

"Poor training, my eye. Everyone in the stadium saw that little girl guide him back to where he belonged with nothing more than voice commands," said another man. "The article also didn't mention that."

"Of course, the article was written by the Royal Society for the Prevention of Cruelty to Animals," said Morys. "The RSPCA has been a long-time opponent of using horses in the collieries."

"It makes me wonder how they heat their homes," said the first.

"They don't know enough about coal mining to be able to offer any alternatives," Morys said. "No question about it, coal mining is dangerous for both man and beast. We all know men who have died. We all know horses who have died. I don't have to tell you that's the risks we take to put food on our tables. And the sacrifices we make to bring energy to all the homes and factories. But they write these articles without ever having been down in the mines to see how well our horses are cared for."

Bethan crept to the front of the stall and peeked over the short wall, listening.

"They claim the pit ponies at the show are not representative of the rest of our ponies," a short man with a mustache said.

Morys shrugged his shoulders. "Well, we ostlers all brought our finest horses to the show, that be true. But so do the hunter/jumper people."

A knowing chuckle flowed through the group.

"But," Morys continued, "I'm proud of the condition of all the pit ponies I'm responsible for. I'd be happy to show any one of them."

Words of agreement came from the other two men.

"Well, I for one," said a tall, thin man wearing a tweed coat, "hope the protests the article called for don't show up and ruin the show for our horses and hauliers. That would be such a shame, especially for that young girl you've brought along."

As Bethan was about to learn, the protests would come in a different and unexpected form.

Chapter 29

ethan's class for large pit ponies was not scheduled until the morning of the following day. Except for taking Dobbin on a walk around the barn and grounds, she had the day to herself. She planned to spend it helping Abigail get ready for her class. Her new friend would be riding in the pony hunter class for children 12 to 18. They agreed to meet at noon at Hardy's stall.

Bethan walked past row after row of box stalls. The stalls were created out of temporary panels assembled next to one another. Unless you had the money to buy two stalls where the center wall could be removed, each horse was housed in a stall that was ten feet by ten feet. It seemed most of the stalls were occupied by fancy thoroughbreds, polished, braided, and ready to show.

"Bethan," Abigail called out.

Bethan turned, looked down the nearest row of stalls, and noticed her friend waving to her. She hurried past tack trunks and blankets, hay bales and feed buckets, until she reached where Abigail was standing.

"Bethan," Abigail gushed. "I didn't get to talk to you yesterday. You were amazing. Dobbin listened to your every word. I hope they caught that mean man who hurt him. Is Dobbin okay?"

"I think it scared him more than hurt him, though he does have a small cut."

"Oh, no. Will that ruin his chances?"

Bethan shrugged. "I hope not. We got it cleaned up quite well. Besides," she continued as she stroked Hardy's soft chestnut coat, "judges are accustomed to seeing nicks and scars on pit ponies. They wouldn't believe they really worked in the mines if they didn't have anything to show for it."

"You know, Dobbin wasn't the only target of the protests. All the pit ponies were," Abigail said.

"I think the target is really all the collieries that use the horses to help in the mines," Bethan said.

"Yes. That makes more sense. I'm sorry you and Dobbin were the ones who got attacked."

Bethan began brushing Hardy's short coat while Abigail polished the tall, black, riding boots she planned to wear. As they worked, they shared stories about their homes and families. The two girls had little in common beyond their love of horses, yet that was enough to build a strong bond.

A half-hour before Abigail's class, Hardy was tacked up and ready to go. Bethan helped Abigail put on her blue show coat and her black velvet-covered riding cap. Her pale-yellow riding breeches billowed at her thighs before narrowing over her knees and disappearing into her boots. Around her neck was a smart white stock tie held in place with a gold pin.

Standing beside her pony, she said, "How do we look?"

"Fabulous. I wish my friend Dylan was here with his camera. I'd have him take a picture of you."

Abigail giggled with delight as she lifted her left leg and placed her shiny boot in the silver stirrup. With a bounce, she was up and settled in the saddle.

Bethan followed her to the warm-up arena where Abigail's instructor was waiting for her. Bethan noticed the girl with the white pony was already in the ring, trotting her pony around. When she saw Abigail and Bethan, she pulled her pony to a stop. "Oh, it's that tip girl. I noticed your performance yesterday at the parade. Seems you can't stay out of the dirt."

"Why must you be so nasty?" Abigail said.

"What did I say? I just told the truth," she said before kicking her pony and trotting off.

"I'm sorry I always have to apologize for her," Abigail said.

"You don't need to. I'm proud of being a tip girl," Bethan said. And for perhaps the first time, she realized she really was.

Abigail's trainer called her over and the two conversed in the middle of the arena. Then Abigail warmed Hardy up with walks, trots, and canters, before taking a few jumps.

After that, the art of keeping him warm without wearing him out began as they waited for her number to be called.

◆ ◆ ◆ ◆ ◆ ◆ ◆ ◆ ◆ ◆

The entire afternoon, Bethan watched the pony hunter classes. The beautiful ponies were so different from the pit ponies she knew and loved. The brave little creatures carried their riders over the jumps without hesitation. Bethan couldn't help but feel just the tiniest twinge of jealousy as she wished she had the chance to ride like that. She shrugged her shoulders and sighed. *Maybe someday,* she thought.

By the end of the day, Abigail had placed in two classes and had a sixth-place ribbon and an eighth-place ribbon to hang on Hardy's stall. The white pony in the next stall had two blue ribbons. Abigail and Bethan didn't care.

Chapter 30

The next day, December 1938

Bethan and her parents ran through the rain to reach the barn. The clouds were so heavy they seemed to be sitting on the ground.

She shivered from the wet and cold as she pulled the barn door open. But entering the barn filled her with excitement. Compared to the winter weather outside, it was warm and dry inside, and the barn was filled with activity. The surroundings buzzed with a familiar vibrancy. The sound of horses stomping with impatience, waiting for their breakfast, was combined with the banging of metal buckets and people talking and laughing.

The section where the pit ponies were stabled was the busiest of all. Today was their big day. It was their chance to show the other collieries and ostlers their best horses and their skill as horsemen. And beyond that, it was their chance to show the world how well the pit ponies were cared for.

As Bethan walked to Dobbin's stall, she heard much discussion about the article in *The Times*. They had all sacrificed much to be here, and they hoped no protesters would show up to ruin their big day.

Bethan began singing her lullaby to calm her nerves.

Close your eyes, little one,
'neath the Welsh moon's gentle glow,
In the meadow where the ponies
softly wander to and fro.
Hush now, dear child,
let the night breeze gently sigh,
As the stars above tell tales of ponies trotting by.

Dobbin heard her and nickered as he stood looking between the bars of his stall.

By this time in the show season, Bethan and Morys had their routine set, and they were able to get Dobbin ready quickly. Soon, Bethan was dressed in her best dress that her mother had cleaned after the debacle during the parade. She led Dobbin out of his stall wearing a clean, leather headstall. They went to the warm-up arena, to wait for their class to be called. Bethan led Dobbin past the colorful jumps.

"What do you think, boy. Could you lift that big body over those jumps?" she jokingly asked. She heard her name and turned to see Abigail waving from the side of the arena.

She led Dobbin over to her friend.

"He looks beautiful," Abigail said, slipping Dobbin a sugar cube. "And so do you. Are you nervous?"

Bethan wanted to appear confident, but she couldn't help herself. "I'm scared to death!"

Abigail laughed. "You wouldn't be a real horsewoman if you weren't!"

The announcer called for the class. Abigail stepped away from the railing. "Good luck!"

Bethan mouthed "Thank you," as she led Dobbin to line up with the others in her class.

Several men leading horses stared at her as she passed. A wrinkled brow here, narrowed eyes there, a set jaw or arms folded across a chest, all told Bethan they were surprised to see her and, perhaps, a bit suspicious. Sure, many had seen her at the parade, but no one expected she would be one of the competitors. Only the hauliers from her area in South Wales who had seen her at the local shows were undaunted by her appearance.

"What's a girl doing here?" she heard one man say.

"Why is she allowed to compete?" said another.

Bethan clenched her jaw, lifted her chin, and kept walking until she found her place in line. She entered the arena behind a large, brown-and-white pit pony from one of the collieries near Penallta. This gave her a small sense of security, knowing that the haulier was one of Morys' friends.

The judges, with clipboards in hand, watched the line of horses enter and stop along the center of the arena. Bethan looked up at the glass ceiling. Rivers of water flowed down the sides as the storm outside continued. Glad to be inside and out of the cold, she smiled and looked around. The seating, arranged like an amphitheater all around the arena, was only half full. But that still meant hundreds of people had braved the elements to watch the pit ponies. She straightened her hat and forced a smile on her face. "We've done this before, Dobbin," she whispered. "We can do it again."

The judges took their time examining each horse, not looking for the same qualities they would in a fancy dressage horse or jumper. For a pit pony, they were looking for strong bones and good muscling in both the shoulders and hind quarters. Thick bones and sturdy hooves were an advantage for a pit pony.

At last, the judges arrived to examine Dobbin.

"Well, well," said the head judge. "I wasn't expecting a girl to be the handler from the Penallta Colliery."

"Yes, sir," said Bethan.

"Do you actually work with him at the mine?"

Bethan hesitated, wondering if she should admit to violating the prohibition of females working in the mines. *What will the judge say if he thinks about the law? Will he disqualify Dobbin?* Quickly, she decided to take her chances with the truth.

"Yes, sir. He was my father's partner until a cave-in broke Tad's legs. I took a break from school and worked his shift in the mine until he recovered."

"I must say, you did an excellent job taking care of his pit pony."

"Thank you, sir," Bethan said, a blush coloring her cheeks, her shoulders dropping in relief.

When they moved on to the next horse, Bethan let out a long breath of air and lifted her hand to rub Dobbin's neck.

It seemed the entire day had passed before the judges gathered at the megaphone to announce the ten finalists, even though it had only been half an hour. As each horse was called, his handler led him to line up facing the judges. Soon there were two horses. Then three, four, five. Bethan felt a shiver run down her spine. She took a deep breath and bit her lower lip, trying to remain hopeful. The sixth horse was the brown-and-white horse in front of her. Then the seventh and eighth horses were called. Nine horses were called out of the line before Bethan heard, "And our last finalist is the entry from the Penallta Colliery."

Bethan was not cognizant of the cheers that went up from the audience. All she was aware of was her body moving mechanically toward the judges and her horse moving beside her. Tears welled in her eyes as she looked at Dobbin. Rubbing his neck, she said, "See, I told you, you could do it."

Chapter 31

Later that day

The finals were to start at four in the afternoon and would require the use of the tram and harness as they had done at the small shows. Bethan and Abigail were in Dobbin's stall, brushing him and touching up his braids when a group of men gathered outside his stall. Bethan recognized the judges from the morning competition. Along with them was Morys and her father, and two other men she didn't recognize.

The girls looked at each other, their eyes wide. Bethan placed her finger to her lips and Abigail nodded in understanding.

"Thank you for meeting us here," the head judge said.

"Of course," said Morys. "What seems to be the problem?"

"We have had a formal complaint filed against our selection of your pit pony as one of the ten finalists," said the judge.

Bethan gasped and held her breath. She noticed her father straighten and place his fisted hands on his hips. Abigail reached over and grabbed Bethan's arm.

"What is the nature of the complaint?" asked Morys, his voice strained.

"Several of the ostlers and hauliers object to a girl in the event."

The two girls turned and looked into one another's eyes but didn't make a sound.

"What could be the reason for their objection?" Morys said, his voice now high-pitched and tense.

"They argue that since it is against the law for girls to be working underground as a haulier, they shouldn't be allowed to show a pit pony. They want the Penallta mine entry disqualified."

No one responded for a few minutes.

Then Morys said, "I see . . . And what say you?"

The judge shuffled his feet. "Well, it seems to me that since the first part of the judging process was only to evaluate the pit pony, and he *is* a pit pony after all, and we judged him solely based on his qualities for the job, I think it only makes sense to let the selections stand as they are."

The two men that Bethan didn't recognize started to object. "But sir, you can't be serious."

The judge held up his hand and gave them a stern look. "That is my decision in the matter. However, there remains the question of the final part of the class to be held in a few hours."

Again, silence. Again, Bethan and Abigail stared at one another, frozen in place.

The judge cleared his throat and adjusted his tweed sport coat and bow tie. When he spoke, it was with a new air of authority, leaving no room for discussion. "Since the second part of the competition deals with the training of the pit pony and how well he works with the haulier, I will ban the girl from competing. If you have another haulier here who can work with the horse, I'll allow him to stay in the competition."

The two strangers walked away grumbling.

Bethan slid down the wall of the stall until she was sitting on the straw bedding. Bringing her knees to her chest, she buried her head and sobbed. Abigail sat beside her, her arm around her shoulders.

Dobbin shuffled over until he was standing directly over her. He lowered his head and wiggled his top lip through her hair.

The stall door slid open, and Thomas peeked his head into the stall. Stepping inside, he kneeled in front of Bethan and took her hands. She looked up, tears streaming down her cheeks.

"You heard what was said, no doubt?" Thomas asked.

Bethan sniffed and nodded her head.

"Then why so sad? Dobbin still gets to compete after all."

"But not with me."

"Is this about you? Or is this about Dobbin?"

Bethan sniffed again and angrily brushed the tears from her cheeks. "I know it's supposed to be about Dobbin, but I kind of thought of us as a team."

"Ahhhh. I see. So, it is really about both of you."

Bethan nodded and sniffled a third time.

"I can see that," Thomas said, sitting down next to her on the opposite side from Abigail. "A team, just like Abigail and her pony."

Bethan nodded again. Abigail dropped her chin as a tear rolled down her own cheek.

Thomas sighed. "You know, my little peach, sometimes fathers can't give their children everything they want, as hard as they may try. This is something I don't have any control over."

"I know," Bethan said, rubbing her eyes.

"We're lucky Dobbin knows me," her father added. "He may not love me as much as he loves you, but he'll at least work with me. I will do my best to make you proud of both Dobbin and me."

Bethan turned and threw her arms around her father's neck. "Oh, Tad! I know you will. Dobbin loves you, too."

◆ ◆ ◆ ◆ ◆ ◆ ◆ ◆ ◆

After Morys, Thomas, and Bethan placed the harness over Dobbin's neck and across his broad back, they attached the shaft to the tram with the limber pin. Thomas straightened and said, "Go on." Dobbin looked back and forth between Thomas and Bethan, then almost seemed to shrug his shoulders before stepping forward.

Abigail took Bethan's hand and led her friend to a seat right in the front row. Catrin joined them.

"This is so exciting," Abigail said. "I've never seen the pit pony competition before this morning. That part of the competition looked just like any other breed class, just with bigger, stronger horses. But this with the trams . . . it's just amazing."

"You girls have Dobbin looking so beautiful," Catrin said. "I'm proud of you."

"Abigail was a big help," Bethan said, trying her best to push down the disappointment that was still eating at her. Turning to Abigail she said, "Meeting you has been the best part about coming to the show."

Abigail hugged her new friend. "I feel the same about you," she said. "We must become pen pals."

Bethan beamed. "Yes, we must." She gave her new friend a smile before turning her attention back to the arena.

Just as he had so many times before in the mine, Thomas walked beside Dobbin, this time as they entered the arena when their names were announced. He memorized the course they were to take between and through the obstacles as the judges gave their instructions.

When it was their turn, Thomas looked over at Bethan where she sat perched on the edge of her seat. He gave her a wink and tipped his hat.

Bethan steepled her hands in front of her mouth and smiled.

"Go on," Thomas said. They started the course. As Thomas walked beside Dobbin in the deep sandy footing, the injuries he suffered in the mine caused him to limp. He gritted his teeth against the pain, determined to see this through. "Gun on," Thomas said when they came to the first obstacle, a tram filled with coal. Dobbin turned left. Step by step, Thomas's voice guided Dobbin through the obstacles until they reached the end. The crowd cheered at the flawless performance.

When Thomas went back in line with the other teams, he glanced over at his family. Bethan and Catrin were radiant. He looked across the arena and noticed that the men who had filed the complaint didn't look quite so happy.

When the judges announced the winner, no one was surprised that Thomas and Dobbin received the blue ribbon. But then, the crowd was stunned as

Thomas unhooked the tram, took off the harness, and led Dobbin to where Bethan sat. "Climb aboard," he said.

Bethan jumped up, climbed onto the short wall, and mounted her pit pony. The victory lap was one to remember as Bethan sat proudly upon Dobbin and waved to the cheering crowd.

Chapter 32

It was on one of those rare, sunny December days, when the silver-blue winter sky seems to go on forever, that Morys pulled the horsebox into the yard. Bethan and her family sighed in relief, glad to be home and freed from the cramped pickup truck.

Dylan had been waiting for them on their front porch. He leaped to his feet when they arrived. Waving wildly, he called, "You're home!"

Bethan jumped out of the cab of the pickup truck. "Dobbin won! Dobbin won," she shouted. "I wish you could have been there."

"So do I," Dylan said. "I would have taken your picture. I want to hear all about it."

As Dylan helped Bethan take care of Dobbin, she told him all that happened at the show, from the Parade of Pit Ponies to the final victory lap. "And I made a new friend. She has the most beautiful pony. We promised to write each other every month."

Once word of Dobbin's return home reached the villagers, they set to work. As jubilant cheers echoed through the streets, the normally stoic village of Hengoed burst into a spontaneous celebration, its vibrant energy palpable. Colorful banners were strung up on every corner, fluttering in the breeze, proudly declaring Hengoed as the cherished abode of "Dobbin the Pit Pony." The pride of Dobbin's triumph radiated throughout the small town; a community tied together by the Penallta Colliery. Smiles on every face and hands waving and clapping showed the profound sense of unity and accomplishment felt in every heart. It was a victory for all of them.

◆ ◆ ◆ ◆ ◆ ◆ ◆ ◆ ◆ ◆

Monday came just two days after their homecoming, and with it, a return to normalcy in a sense. For Bethan, it meant a return to the Hengoed County Girls' School. For Dobbin, it meant a return to the coal mine. Bethan watched her father lead him away into the darkness. She sighed and pursed her lips to keep the tears at bay.

Thomas walked beside Dobbin all the way to the colliery and into the wood-covered cage at the top of the pit. The horses at the windlass walked in their well-worn circle and lowered Dobbin back down the pit to his old home. For Dobbin, even the glory of winning didn't mean a change of job or lifestyle.

Bethan threw herself back into her schoolwork. Her time with Dobbin and the shows had done nothing to diminish her dream of going to the university and becoming a veterinarian. If anything, her goal was clearer than ever.

But each day, she made her father report on Dobbin's condition. On one such day, she asked, "How was Dobbin today, Tad?"

"Oh, he had a rough go of it today."

Bethan looked up from her plate, her brows knitted. "What do you mean?"

"He hooked his shoe on the rail and pulled it off," Thomas said, buttering a piece of bread.

"Is he lame now?"

"Oh, no. He'll be fine. Luckily it was the farrier's day to come down the pit. He fixed him right up. Please pass the jam."

"What would have happened if the farrier hadn't been there?" asked Bethan, still concerned.

"Well, I would have had to take him off work until the shoe was replaced. We really can't work the ponies on that rough ground without protection for their hooves."

So, even though Bethan missed Dobbin terribly, she was glad her father was there to take care of him.

Over the next year, her father assured and reassured her he was doing well at his job.

Even though no other pit pony could take Dobbin's place, periodically, Thomas brought home a horse that needed doctoring. This gave Bethan a chance to be with the horses and gain more veterinary knowledge.

Meanwhile, Dylan continued to work hard at the mine and spent many evenings working with his uncle on his woodworking skills. When time permitted, Bethan and Dylan spent time together sharing their dreams.

All seemed good until . . .

Chapter 33

Hengoed, September 1939

ylan's uncle had a radio in his woodshop. As Dylan worked, he and his uncle listened to the news broadcast by the BBC, the British Broadcasting Corporation. On September 1, 1939, Dylan was sanding a piece of wood destined to become a table leg when the broadcaster announced the shocking news that Germany had invaded Poland in what was called a "Blitzkrieg"—a large and damaging surprise military attack. According to the announcement, France and Britain were demanding that Germany immediately withdraw, or else . . .

Dylan and his uncle stopped work and looked at one another. "Or else what?" Dylan asked.

"I don't know," his uncle said. "But I don't like the sound of this."

Two days later, Britain and France declared war on Germany and World War II had begun.

◆ ◆ ◆ ◆ ◆ ◆ ◆ ◆ ◆ ◆

For Wales, as well as the rest of Great Britain— and frankly the entire world—life changed immediately.

In the tumult of World War II, every able-bodied man in Britain aged 18 to 41 faced the looming prospect of military conscription, unless they were engaged in a "Reserved Occupation" critical to the war effort. Among these vital roles was coal mining, a cornerstone of Hengoed's livelihood, sparing its men from the draft's immediate grip. Yet, this exemption was not unique to Hengoed alone; it echoed across the rugged valleys of South Wales, where collieries hummed with activity and resilience.

However, despite the relief of exemption for some villages, the specter of war cast its shadow over all of Wales. By the war's culmination, a staggering 300,000 Welsh souls, both men and women, had answered the call to arms. Tragically, the cost of this sacrifice was steep, with an estimated 15,000 lives lost in the line of duty. Thus, across every corner of Wales, worry and prayers intertwined. Each community held a personal stake in the tumult of war as loved ones were thrust into the expanding conflict.

As the fighting increased, coal emerged as an essential source of power for factories and the relentless engines of war. This propelled Thomas and Dobbin into a demanding work schedule.

Their toil fed the ceaseless hunger for coal. Therefore, all the miners and pit ponies were forced to labor for extended hours under the dim glow of their headlamps.

In the heart of the coal-laden earth, Thomas and Dobbin strengthened their partnership. With expertise born of patience and skill, they wove their way through the labyrinthine tunnels. Soon their capability became a beacon in the dark mines for those, newly recruited to mining, learned under their tutelage. It wasn't merely about mastering the art of hauling coal; it was about forging an unbreakable bond between coal miners and these majestic creatures. In these perilous depths, men and horses toiled side by side forging an enduring spirit of partnership.

While Thomas and Dobbin toiled for long hours far below ground, Catrin did her best to keep the home running smoothly. Bethan stayed in school focusing on fulfilling her dream to study at a university.

An unforeseen benefit, not realized at the time, was that Hengoed and the other mines in the valleys of South Wales were ensured the progress fueled by coal would burn brightly for many years to come. The influx of wealth from the coal industry not only bolstered the local economy, but also banished the specter of unemployment that once loomed over all of South Wales.

While there were shortages of food and clothing, for some of the poorest people in South Wales, the job opportunities actually improved their lives. Many were eating better than they had for years, even with rationing.

Because of their demanding schedule, Bethan rarely got to see her father or Dylan, as they were forced to work every day, including on the Sabbath. Some mornings, she got up early to have breakfast with her father and walk with Dylan part of the way to the colliery. She cherished those few minutes of time with them.

Thomas and Dylan walked home together at night, the black-out orders making the trek to the village dark and dreary. But everyone understood the necessity. Nearly a thousand Welsh civilians were killed in air raids – primarily around Cardiff. Cardiff was the major port for shipping coal to Europe. Since Cardiff was so close to Hengoed, the villagers lived in constant fear.

Understanding the necessity or not, the darkness seemed oppressive.

On a rare clear night, Thomas looked up at the full moon and said, "What a welcome sight the moon is tonight, don't you think, Dylan?"

Dylan pursed his lips as he considered his answer. "It's like a white sun in a black sky."

"The only sun we get to see," added Thomas.

Dylan stopped and turned to Thomas. "I don't want to spend my life underground."

Thomas nodded, his eyes downcast. "I understand."

"I have dreams just as Bethan does," Dylan added.

Thomas turned to Dylan and placed his blackened hands on the teen's shoulders. He looked him in the eye and said, "Then you must reach for those dreams. Don't let anything stop you."

* * * * * * * * * *

With many men drafted for the war and sent to Europe, rules governing women working in mines and factories were loosened. New munitions factories were built in Hirwaun, Glascoed, and Bridgend. They employed 60,000 workers, most of them women. Many of Catrin's friends started working in one of the factories in Hirwaun, being only 16 miles away. They could take the bus to and from work.

One night, Bethan lay in bed, listening to her parents talking downstairs.

"Alys has started working at the munitions factory in Hirwaun," she heard her mother say.

"Huh," her father grunted.

"Did you know she is bringing home more money than her husband is?"

"What?"

"It's true," Catrin said.

"That's nice," Thomas said.

"I was thinking about going to see if they had a job I could do, even with my leg braces."

Bethan heard the silverware drop.

"No. I won't have it," Thomas shouted, and then coughed several times.

"Shhhh," Catrin said. "You'll wake Bethan."

"I don't want you working in a factory," Thomas said, softer this time.

"But think what a boon it would be. We wouldn't have to worry about school tuition for Bethan anymore. And we could save for her university studies."

"We are managing just fine now. And with the extra money I'm earning, we'll be able to help her go to the university."

Thomas had another coughing spell.

"But I worry about you. Your cough seems to be getting worse. And what if there was another accident in the mine?"

"We need you here in our home, taking care of us," Thomas said, his voice filled with tenderness.

"Perhaps you could find some volunteer work here in Hengoed to help with the war effort."

Bethan rolled over in her bed and covered her head with her quilt. Would this war never end? Or was it just the beginning?

❖ ❖ ❖ ❖ ❖ ❖ ❖ ❖ ❖ ❖

The next morning, Bethan approached her parents as they sat at breakfast. "Mam, Tad, I am going to return to work at the mine on my days off from school."

Both of her parents looked up in surprise.

"That isn't necessary, my little peach," said Thomas. "We're doing just fine with the increase in my salary from the longer working hours.

"I want to be able to start saving for my university studies," Bethan said. "I heard the mine was short of hauliers."

"Morys, Dobbin, and I have been trying to teach the new boys and ponies as quickly as we can," Thomas interjected.

"But *I* don't need training. I think with so many women and girls working in the war effort, the manager might take me back as a haulier. Besides, I miss Dobbin."

Thomas smiled. "And he misses you."

Catrin turned to her husband. "What do you think, Thomas? Would the manager take her back?"

Thomas shrugged. "He knows you and Dobbin make a good team. They've taken several women in the office and other above ground jobs. I think the threat of hefty fines for allowing women to work underground is minimal. If Bethan wants to do this, we'll just have to see what he says."

Chapter 34

The manager of the Penallta mine, feeling the pressure to produce more and more coal, was an easy sell. The coming Saturday, Bethan walked to the mine with her father and Dylan. She rode down the pit in the familiar cage. As she did so, she felt her heart beating in anticipation of what she knew was coming. When the cage hit the bottom of the pit with a jolt, she bit her lip and grinned. Squeezing Dylan's hand, she said, "Why do I feel like I'm back home?"

Dylan could only laugh. "Someday we'll have a home, but it won't be like this, I can promise you that!"

Entering the mine, she immediately noticed some changes. Electric lights now extended all the way to the stables—a welcome improvement.

Bethan reached the familiar stables with the horse's names painted on each stall. She started singing her lullaby.

Dobbin's head appeared over the brick wall that bordered his stall, ears twitching back and forth.

"Dobbin," Bethan cried as she reached his stall. "Oh, Dobbin. I'm back."

"Well, look who's back." Bethan turned to see Morys walking up the aisle toward her. "Glad to see ye, lass," he said, giving Bethan a hug and a rap on her helmet.

"Thanks, Morys. I've actually missed you."

"Naw. Ye can't fool me. Ye just missed yer horse!"

Bethan found herself enjoying being back in the familiar bustle of the stables surrounded by fellow hauliers preparing their pit ponies for another day below ground. The air was thick with the earthy scent of hay and leather. The sound of hooves clattering against the cobblestones was music to her ears.

Thomas readied a red-roan gelding appropriately named Roany, while Dylan prepared a large black and white gelding named Seville. As the last buckles were fastened and the final checks completed, the trio joined the other hauliers as they ventured into the darkness of the tunnels.

◆ ◆ ◆ ◆ ◆ ◆ ◆ ◆ ◆

Month after month, Bethan joined her father and Dylan on her days off from school, working far underground hauling trams of coal to the pit to be brought up to the surface. The rats no longer worried her, though she still didn't like them and knew she never would, and she was careful to keep her gas lamp lit. She ended each day washing the coal dust off Dobbin and feeding him his dinner.

Even with her special care, Dobbin and all the other pit ponies were losing weight. Between the extra hours of work and the poor quality of hay and oats they were allotted, there was nothing that could be done. Humans and animals were all feeling the consequences of the war.

It was a dark February day when Bethan felt the first tinges of worry. She sensed something was wrong with Dobbin, though she couldn't put her finger on it. He just wasn't the same. As she walked with Dylan to the colliery, she found her mind wrestling with her concerns. She did her best to push them aside and go about her tasks.

Dylan noticed how preoccupied she seemed. "What's bothering you?" he asked.

"Oh . . . nothing," she said.

"Come now. I know you too well. Something is bothering you. You know you can tell me."

"I can't really put my finger on it. I'll talk to you if I get it figured out."

Dylan put his arm around her shoulder. "I'll always be here for you."

Bethan rose up on her toes and kissed his cheek. "I know, and I count on that."

When she got to Dobbin's stall, the horse's welcoming nicker put her mind at ease. *He's fine, just fine,* she told herself.

Bethan went about putting on Dobbin's harness and waved goodbye to her father and Dylan as she led her pony toward the main tunnel. Her assigned coal face was more than a mile away. "Go on," she told Dobbin and, adjusting her gas lamp to shine a beam of light a few feet in front of them, started walking. Dobbin dropped his head and began pulling the empty tram behind her.

They reached the tumble-up in good time, and the miners at the face went about the difficult task of switching the empty tram for the full one.

"Yer all set," one of the miners said as he inserted the limber that connected Dobbin's shaft to the draw bar on the full tram. He wiped the sweat off his forehead with a dirty handkerchief.

"Thank you," Bethan said. "We'll see you again in a couple of hours."

She reached up to rub Dobbin's face and noticed something was wrong. He didn't flinch or blink as her hand neared his eye. She waved her hand back and forth in front of both eyes. He didn't respond. A sick feeling overcame her. The worry that filled her thoughts earlier returned. She had heard of pit ponies going blind, but she couldn't let that happen to Dobbin. *I must be imagining it,* she thought. *We got here just fine.*

"Go on, Dobbin," she said. "Go on." With her lips pressed tightly together, she watched as Dobbin lifted a hoof and placed it down between the rails. Nothing seemed amiss as Dobbin walked forward. Suppressing her fears, she stepped in front of Dobbin and headed back toward the pit.

As they walked, she kept glancing back at Dobbin. He continued to walk forward, his head down, pulling his heavy load of coal. But when they came to the first set of air-doors, Bethan stepped to one side. Dobbin's ears twitched, then he stopped. "Go on, Dobbin," Bethan said. In horror, she watched as Dobbin stepped forward, but when he reached the air-doors, he didn't push them open as he had been taught; he ran right into them, banging his head against the metal doors.

"Oh, Dobbin. Oh, my poor Dobbin," Bethan cried. Her breath burst in and out and her chin trembled. She had been right. There had been something wrong. Dobbin was blind.

What would this mean for her wonderful pit pony? The mine owner wouldn't keep a blind horse around. She approached Dobbin and buried her face in his mane. Her first thoughts were to keep this hidden. She had to protect Dobbin. But she couldn't endanger the other miners and pit ponies. She had heard of blind horses going off the rails and knocking into a support beam, causing a collapse. No. She couldn't do that and risk her father's or Dylan's lives. She had to get Dobbin safely back to the stable and then deal with whatever might happen.

Using voice commands, she directed Dobbin back to the base of the pit, unhooked the full tram, and led him back to the stable.

"What ya doin' back so early, lass," Morys said when he found Bethan in Dobbin's stall undoing his harness.

Bethan looked up, then ran into Morys' arms. The tears she had been holding in for the past hour burst forth.

"Whoa, whoa, lass. It can't be that bad," Morys said, patting her back as she clung to him. "Tell me what's wrong."

"D-Dobbin," she stuttered.

"Yes. Dobbin."

"Dobbin's b-blind."

Morys stiffened. He gently removed Bethan's arms from around his waist and walked up to Dobbin's head. He waved his hands in front of the near-side eyeball, then the off-side eye. Dobbin didn't respond. He didn't flinch. He didn't even blink.

Morys dropped his chin and shook his head. He knew what this meant. Dobbin would have to go.

Chapter 35

Penallta Colliery, winter 1941

When a pit pony is no longer able to do his job, there are only two options. The pony is euthanized, or the pony is given to someone who will take care of him.

For Dobbin, Bethan would only accept the latter option. She would be the one who would care for him for the rest of his life.

Bethan and Dylan spent the next couple of days preparing the paddock for Dobbin.

"Let's start by cutting away all the low-hanging branches from the trees near the fence," Bethan said. 'I wouldn't want him to run into them."

"We better check every fence board for risen nails, splinters, or sharp points," added Dylan.

"We're good at raking," joked Bethan as she grabbed a rake. "Let's make sure the ground is clear." The pasture was raked to ensure there was nothing that could hurt him.

Thomas filled the little shed with hay and grain and purchased a new water tank that was free of sharp or rusty edges.

When all was prepared at home, Bethan and Thomas went down in the pit and helped the miners attach wooden boards to the sides of the cage for protection.

When all was ready, Thomas took Bethan's hand and walked with her to Dobbin's stall. As they approached, Bethan stopped and gazed at Dobbin's name painted above his stall. She sighed. "I guess they'll remove that."

Thomas nodded. "He may not have a job to do anymore, but he'll have a happy home."

Bethan smiled, turned, and hugged her father. "Thank you, Tad, for letting us keep him."

"There's nowhere else he belongs," Thomas said as he gave her hand a squeeze.

With one on either side, they led Dobbin to the cage. Using soothing voices, they directed him onto the platform and watched as Dobbin was lifted out of the mine for the last time.

Chapter 36

Hengoed, *spring* 1942

*H*aving endured two and a half years since the beginning of World War II, Bethan and her friends and family learned to structure their lives and society around ceaseless war. Life as they had known it in their little valley seemed to be gone forever. The smokestacks at the colliery continued to spew forth their dark clouds of smoke day and night. But that seemed to be the only constant.

Schools struggled to stay open for lack of teachers. Stores sat half empty. Churches offered comfort to the few who were able to attend. Festivals and holidays were cancelled and no longer added color to their mundane existence. That's just how things were in Hengoed.

The one source of escape from it all was the cinema. Bethan and Dylan took advantage of the few days he had off from the mine, immersing themselves in the darkened theater and watching a movie.

"I don't know why you go to those movies," Thomas said one day.

"Why, Tad?" Bethan asked. "It's a fun way to relax. You should come with us."

Thomas shook his head. "I won't subject myself to that government propaganda," he said, referring to the news reels that proceeded every film. "To me, it is very un-British-like to be pushing all those pro-war half-truths, trying to get people all riled up. It seems more appropriate for that to be coming from the Fascist countries we're trying to fight."

Bethan pondered her father's words and asked Dylan what he thought.

"We have to stop the Third Reich, or they'll take over the world," Dylan said.

"But do you think we're being told the truth?" Bethan said.

"Of course, we are," Dylan said. "Why would our government lie to us?"

◆ ◆ ◆ ◆ ◆ ◆ ◆ ◆ ◆

Bethan finished her schooling at Hengoed County Girls' School at the end of May. Her mother had saved up her sugar coupons and baked a cake. When

Thomas and Dylan arrived home from working in the colliery, they gathered together to celebrate.

Once the cake was gone, Dylan produced a package wrapped with old newspaper and tied with string. "Open it," he said, pushing it toward her.

"Oh, Dylan," Bethan said with a giggle. "You shouldn't have."

"It's just something I made. I hope you like it."

Bethan untied the string and set it aside to save; nothing useful was thrown away. She unfolded the paper. Looking down, she gasped. Sitting on the ruffled paper was the most beautiful wooden jewelry box she had ever seen. Different types of wood were inlaid into a heart pattern and sanded until the top was as smooth as silk. She gently opened the lid. The inside was lined with purple velvet, and sitting on the soft fabric was a silver sixpence.

She looked up at Dylan, her mouth open, her eyes wide. She couldn't find the words to say.

Dylan smiled. "I made this box for you. And the sixpence is my contribution to your university schooling. It isn't much, but..."

Bethan set the box on the table and threw her arms around Dylan. "It's the most beautiful thing I've ever seen. Thank you, so much. I will treasure it forever."

◆ ◆ ◆ ◆ ◆ ◆ ◆ ◆ ◆

Over the next few days, Bethan noticed that Dylan was not his usual jovial self. As they took Dobbin for walks through the wildflower fields that dotted the valley, he said little. She glanced over at him, but he avoided looking at her. At last, she could stand it no longer. She grabbed his hand and stopped him in mid-stride. "Tell me what's bothering you," she pleaded.

"I don't know how to tell you," he said, looking down at the waving grasses that surrounded them. He reached over and stroked Dobbin's neck as the horse stretched down to nibble on some grass.

"Whatever it is, just say it. We've been friends too long to keep secrets from one another."

Dylan took a deep breath. The words rushed out. "I've enlisted in the army."

Stunned, Bethan dropped his hand.

"See. I knew you'd be upset," Dylan said.

"B-but why?" Bethan stammered. "You are working in the mine. That's a reserved occupation. You don't have to go to war."

Dylan turned and faced her. Looking her in the eyes, he said, "I need to do this. People are dying to preserve my freedom—to preserve your freedom."

"But you're already helping the war effort by producing the coal they need," she said, her voice pleading. "And now Tad has taught you to be a haulier; you get to work with the pit ponies."

"I know. But it's not enough. I feel I have more to offer."

Tears welled up in Bethan's eyes.

Dylan took her in his arms and held her tightly while she cried. He stroked her hair and whispered in her ear, "I will return. I promise."

Chapter 37

A few miles north of Caerphilly, South
Wales, August 1997

The sun dropped down, kissing the horizon, and turning the clouds pink and gold. The giant earthmovers rumbled to a stop; the work completed for the day.

Quinn looked up at her grandmother. "What happened next, Mamgu?" she asked.

"Oh, sweet Quinn," Grandmother said. "I went off to the university to become a vet, and your grandfather went off to the war."

"And then?" she asked, her eyes beseeching.

Grandmother chuckled and put her arm around Quinn. "I think you know the rest of the story. Grandfather came home when the war ended and became the best cabinet maker in the valley. We married and started our family. I have spent my life caring for my children and the animals in our village."

Grandmother kissed her granddaughter on the forehead. "And now we have you."

"But Dobbin? What happened to Dobbin?"

Grandmother looked over at the sunset. Her eyes softened and a distant, unfocused smile crossed her lips. Her hand went to her neck around which hung a silver sixpence on a chain. She rubbed it lovingly. When she spoke, her voice was quiet.

"Dobbin lived the rest of his days in our paddock. Even blind, he seemed happy." Grandmother chuckled at the memories flooding her mind. "He followed me around like your puppy does you, using his ears to guide him."

Quinn looked up at the sky. "Look, Mamgu," she said, her voice filled with excitement. She pointed to a cloud formation directly over them. "It's Dobbin."

Grandmother followed Quinn's gaze. The night stars were just starting to appear. And moving between the stars was a large cloud that looked like a running horse. "It is indeed. It must be Dobbin watching over us now as he always did."

Quinn took her grandmother's hand and grinned. "As the stars above tell tales of ponies trotting by."

M.J. Evans

A History of Horses Underground - Notes from the Author

For centuries, horses have been involved in bringing coal from where it lay dormant in the ground to homes and factories around the world. The earliest records of using coal as a burning agent date back to China in 3490 BC. It wasn't until the start of the Industrial Revolution at the beginning of the eighteenth century that coal mining became a large and essential operation. That was when horses became a necessary part of mining and delivering coal.

The first job horses fulfilled was to haul loads of coal away from the mines and take them to where it was needed: homes and factories. They were also employed on the windlasses, bringing trams of coal up from underground.

As the demand for coal increased and mining technology improved, horses were taken down the mine itself to provide the power needed to haul large quantities of coal. Before that, children as young as eight pulled out carts of coal while crawling through the low, narrow tunnels on their hands and knees, chained to a wagon.

For more than two hundred years, horses provided the power to bring substantial quantities of coal from the face to the pit bottom. This was called "hauling" in the South of Wales.

All the horses that worked underground, regardless of size, were called "pit ponies." The pit ponies in the south valleys of Wales were usually a mix of Welsh Mountain Ponies and the larger draft breeds such as Shires. It was only in the north that small ponies were used, as the northern coal seams were narrower and the tunnels lower.

In 1878, the Royal Society for the Prevention of Cruelty to Animals (RSPCA) estimated that there were around 200,000 horses working in British mines. But with increased mechanization, this number began to decline. Mechanical conveyors, developed in the early 1900s, proved to be a more rapid way of moving coal. And from 1933 onward, underground locomotives came into use. Still, horses continued to work in the mines. But when the British coal mines were nationalized in 1947, there were only 8,000 horses working in the mines, and most of the collieries in Wales had no horses at all. The last horses working in Welsh mines were finally retired in 1999.

While many of us feel an ache in our hearts at the thought of these beautiful creatures spending their lives in the dirty, dark, damp, underground tunnels of the coal mines, my research indicates that, on the whole, they were well cared for. While most mine owners probably only considered the horses to be a commodity like any other piece of equipment, they were still vital to the success of the mine. Therefore, they needed to be taken care of. Was there animal abuse going on? I have no doubt that when humans are working with animals, there will be occasional abuse. However, mistreatment of the pit ponies was grounds for termination at any of the mines. I found much evidence in my research that most of the hauliers loved and respected their four-legged companions.

There is no question that coal mining was, and still is, a dangerous occupation for both man and horse. Explosions, fires, cave-ins, and equipment accidents all caused severe injuries and even death. The pit ponies were victims of these accidents just as much as the men were. But there are also records of instances where horses saved the lives of the miners. Many hauliers claimed their pit ponies had a sixth sense that warned them of danger. At other times, miners risked their lives to save the ponies.

You might be interested to know that there really were horse shows where the collieries proudly exhibited their pit ponies.

It wasn't until 1842 that age limits were placed on children working in the collieries. At that time, women and girls were banned from working underground. However, I found that the restrictions on using girls and women were mostly ignored. The women would either disguise themselves as men in

Coal miner and pit pony in the Penallta Mine.

Used with permission from 'Big Pit: National Coal Museum',

Blaevanon, Wales

order to get the higher pay, or the managers would ignore the rules in order to have women in the mines who could be paid a lower wage.

As I mentioned earlier, the mine owners had a vested interest in keeping the horses healthy. As a result, many of the largest mines had veterinarians and farriers on staff full-time. The smaller mines would share vets and horseshoers.

In addition, keeping the horses fed was an enormous job. Lowering hay and grain down the pit was done with the same cages that carried the men up and down.

It was fun to learn that, in later years, all the miners were given a two-week paid vacation. And the best part? So were the pit ponies!

The Penallta Mine

Used with permission from 'Big Pit: National Coal Museum', Blaevanon, Wales

Sultan

My inspiration for this book was provided by my daughter, who sent me this captivating picture of "Sultan." This is an arial photograph of the earthen sculpture which was introduced at the onset and conclusion of this book. Erected on the site of the now-closed Penallta Colliery, it was created out of the mountains of coal slag which once defined the area's landscape.

On November 1, 1991, the Penallta mine shuttered its operations, marking the end of an era. It was the last deep working mine in the Rhymney Valley.

In 1996, the local residents opted to transform the area into a park, christening it "The Penallta Country

Park." Besides the bridle paths, cycling trails, boardwalks, forest, wetlands, and lakes, the most remarkable feature is Sultan.

The 200-meter-long earthen sculpture of a running horse was created by artist Mike Petts, using 60,000 tons of coal shale waste. From the ground it merely looks like mounds of grass-covered dirt. It is from the air that Sultan can be seen in all his splendor.

Welsh Terms Used in this Book:

Bait-stand: food break.

Chaff: a mix of chopped hay and oats.

Choppy-box: lunch box.

Grubb-time: lunch break.

Haulier: a miner who works with the pit ponies.

Laverbread: a staple of poor Welsh families made from seaweed. It can be dried then reconstituted into a paste or mixed with oats to make a patty that is fried.

Limber: also called a cotter pin, connects the shaft on the pony's harness to the draw bar on the tram.

Mam: the name for Mother.

Mamgu: the name for Grandmother.

Ostler: the man in charge of caring for the pit ponies in the mine.

Pit ponies: the term for ponies and horses working in the mines.

Riddle: raking the coal to separate it from the culm (dust).

Slag heap: piles of waste from the coal mine.

M.J. Evans

Sprag: a rounded piece of timber with sharp pointed
ends used to jam the wheels of the tram to slow it
down.

Tad: the name for Father.

Tip girls: the name for girls working in the mines of
South Wales.

Tumble up: The area at the coal face where empty
trams are switched for full ones.

Tram: the cart filled with chunks of coal that the pit
ponies pull through the mines. Also called drams.

Windlass: a horse-powered wheel that raises trams
and cages from the pit bottom.

Yorks: strings that the miners tied around their
trousers to keep the rats from crawling up their legs.

Miners and pit ponies at the Penallta Colliery.
Used with permission from the Big Pit National Coal Museum, Wales

Acknowledgements

My thanks to Ceri Thompson of the Big Pit National Coal Museum in Blaevanon, South Wales. He answered all my questions quickly and fully and offered great advice. He met with me on Zoom as well as corresponding by email. I look forward to meeting him in person one day.

No book can be complete until it has been seen by the keen eye of an editor. I am so grateful for Denny Dressman who read each chapter as it was completed and offered his wise council, and for Sophia Barsuhn who looked for any and every error my fingers make on the keyboard.

Bibliography

Bright, John, *Pit Ponies*, 1986, Batsford

Shopland, Norena, *Women in Welsh Coal Mining – Tip Girls at Work in a Men's World*, 2023, Pen and Sword Books

Thompson, Ceri, *Harnessed – Colliery Horses in Wales*, 2008, National Museum Wales Books

ABOUT THE AUTHOR

M.J. Evans is the author of more than twenty award-winning books for middle-graders, young adults, adults, and even a few picture books. Most of her titles are about horses or horse fantasy creatures. Ms. Evans is a graduate of Oregon State University and a former teacher of middle-school and high school students. She is the mother of five and the grandmother of thirteen. She and her husband live in Colorado with their horses and a standard poodle.

Visit her website to learn more about the author and her books!

If you enjoyed this book, please take a minute to post a short review on Amazon. That helps others find the book as well.

You can contact M.J. Evans on her website: www.dancinghorsepress.com She loves to receive letters and she always writes back!

Follow her on social media:

Goodreads:
https://www.goodreads.com/author/show/4496514.M J Evans

Bookbub:

https://www.bookbub.com/profile/m-j-evans

Amazon:

https://www.amazon.com/M.-J.-Evans/e/Boo4GM
So14

Instagram:
https://www.instagram.com/mjevansbooks

Facebook:
https://www.facebook.com/margi.evans.98

Join her **email list** for occasional updates on new releases and receive a FREE PDF of a short Christmas story. Email her at mjevansbtm@gmail.com and put "Join email list" in the subject line.

Read more Award-Winning Titles by M.J. Evans:

Novels:
Coal Dust and Dreams
Finding Fionn
The Stallion and His Peculiar Boy
In the Heart of a Mustang
The Sand Pounder
PINTO!
North Mystic
Mr. Figgletoes' Toy Emporium

Series:
The Mist Trilogy-
Behind the Mist
Mists of Darkness
The Rising Mist

The Centaur Chronicles-
The Stone of Mercy
The Stone of Courage
The Stone of Integrity
The Stone of Wisdom

Picture Books:
Percy-The Racehorse Who Didn't Like to Run
The Skullington Family Series-
Boney Fingers
Bone Appetit
School is a Grave Mistake
Skeletons in the Closet

All titles are available on the website:
www.**dancinghorsepress.com**

And wherever books are sold.